THE FORTUNES OF TEXAS

Follow the lives and loves of a complex family with a rich history and deep ties in the Lone Star State.

THE WEDDING GIFT

The town of Rambling Rose, Texas, is brimming with excitement over the upcoming wedding of five Fortune couples! They're scheduled to tie the knot on New Year's Eve, but one wedding gift arrives early, setting off a mystery that could send shock waves through the entire Fortune family...

Draper Fortune is a reluctant relocator, living in Rambling Rose temporarily and dating up a storm. Ginny Sanders is his homebody next-door neighbor, a sensitive artist and teacher who shies away from relationships. Draper might just be the one to rescue Ginny from her loneliness—or is it the other way around?

Dear Reader,

I've always had a soft spot for opposites-attract stories. She is the yin to his yang, the jelly to his peanut butter, the spring in his formerly plodding step. Their differences awaken and complete one other. They make each other better in the best ways.

In *Cinderella Next Door*, Ginny Sanders has a secret that has kept her locked in her figurative ivory tower (aka her front porch). From there, she watches the world—and her handsome neighbor, Draper Fortune—from a safe distance, dreaming of what it would be like to break out of her shell...and be one of the glamorous women on Draper's arm. The funny thing is none of those glamorous women have had what it takes to make Draper believe in love. With a little help from their fairy godmothers, otherwise known as their meddling relatives and friends, they both realize the past doesn't define them—and discover the courage to fall in love.

I hope you enjoy Ginny and Draper's story as much as I loved writing it. I love to hear from readers, so please let me know your thoughts! You can reach me at nrobardsthompson@yahoo.com.

Warmly,

Nancy

Cinderella Next Door

NANCY ROBARDS THOMPSON

Special thanks and acknowledgment are given to Nancy Robards Thompson for her contribution to The Fortunes of Texas: The Wedding Gift miniseries.

Recycling programs for this product may not exist in your area.

ISBN-13: 978-1-335-40845-7

Cinderella Next Door

For questions and comments about the quality of this book, please contact us at CustomerService@Harlequin.com.

Harlequin Enterprises ULC
22 Adelaide St. West, 41st Floor
Toronto, Ontario M5H 4E3, Canada
www.Harlequin.com

Printed in U.S.A.

Nationally bestselling author **Nancy Robards Thompson** holds a degree in journalism. She worked as a newspaper reporter until she realized reporting "just the facts" bored her silly. Now that she has much more content to report to her muse, Nancy loves writing women's fiction and romance full-time. Critics have deemed her work "funny, smart and observant." She resides in Florida with her husband and daughter. You can reach her at Facebook.com/nrobardsthompson.

Books by Nancy Robards Thompson

Harlequin Special Edition

Celebrations, Inc.

Celebration's Family
Celebration's Baby
A Celebration Christmas
How to Marry a Doctor
His Texas Christmas Bride

The Fortunes of Texas: Rulebreakers

Maddie Fortune's Perfect Man

The Fortunes of Texas: The Secret Fortunes

Fortune's Surprise Engagement

The Fortunes of Texas: Rambling Rose

Betting on a Fortune

Visit the Author Profile page
at Harlequin.com for more titles.

This book is dedicated to my besties—
Kathy, Cindy, Eve, Lenora, Janet, Denise, Kathleen,
Mimi and Jennifer. Your friendship is a gift.

Chapter One

Ginny Sanders stepped back from the easel and surveyed her painting—a riot of roses, hydrangeas and cherry blossoms that she'd gathered from her yard and put into a vase for today's personal painting challenge.

The plan was to knock out a still life in thirty minutes every day for a year.

Every. Single. Day.

No excuses.

She'd set the goal on January first. Today was April first. That meant after she finished this one, she would have completed ninety-one paintings. A swell of accomplishment bloomed in her chest.

The canvases were small—only six by six—but

that was fine. What mattered was that she was showing up at the easel every day.

The painting challenge was part of a bigger plan. On New Year's Eve, as the old year gave way to the new, Ginny had done some soul-searching and decided she couldn't ignore the discontent that had been following her around like a rain cloud.

Last year, she felt…stuck. Stuck in her job. Stuck in her mundane life. The realization had hit her with the power of a tsunami. It was a shame to settle for discontent when she was only twenty-seven years old.

After graduating from college, she'd spent three years working to land a teaching job at Rambling Rose High School. She'd volunteered at the school and accepted last-minute calls to substitute-teach while working afternoons and evenings at Kirby's Perks coffeehouse.

She could've left Rambling Rose to teach at another school, but she didn't want to. This was her hometown.

She knew if she waited long enough, something was bound to open up. And it had. Ginny had eventually gotten the job teaching English after her mother had given up the position, when she and Ginny's father had accepted a teach-abroad opportunity and had moved to Japan to teach English as a second language.

Yep. Miss Sanders had replaced Mrs. Sanders.

Now, just two years after attaining her position

on the Rambling Rose High School faculty, Ginny fought the hollow feeling that this was the best life had to offer.

And it wasn't enough.

On New Year's Eve, she'd been hyperaware of this growing discontent. She'd spent a quiet night at home with her brother Jerry, who was her roommate. He'd also been dateless.

The entire night, she couldn't stop thinking about the elegant Fortune wedding that was unfolding at the Hotel Fortune. While she was at home watching the ball drop on TV, five glamorous couples were tying the knot. She'd never been into fancy affairs or the trappings of wealth, but for some reason, she couldn't stop thinking about the perfect couples who were starting off their lives together.

It seemed symbolic: new year, new life.

That prompted Ginny to lament her general sense of ennui to Jerry, who had diagnosed her with a classic case of, all work and no play made Ginny a very dull girl. "You need to take stock of your life and figure out what's missing."

It had been a good suggestion.

After much self-examination, she'd concluded that she missed painting. She'd painted in high school and into her first semester of college, when she'd quit. Since graduation, she'd pushed painting so far back on her life's back burner, she'd forgotten how much she loved it.

That's why she'd created the painting challenge

and why she was standing on the front porch behind her easel mixing paint, when Draper Fortune's white Tesla turned into his driveway next door.

Her heart leaped and hammered, and she tried to make herself as small as possible behind her easel until she heard his front door shut and she could breathe a sigh of relief. In her paint-splattered clothes, with her brown hair knotted haphazardly on top of her head, she wasn't exactly a picture of loveliness.

She might have had a tiny crush on the guy next door, but the thought of talking to him made her break out in hives.

It hadn't always been this way. In the beginning, he'd wave if he saw her taking out the trash or picking up the mail or painting on the front porch. The hedge between their houses was so high that they either had to be on their porches or meeting at the street for mail or weekly garbage to see each other. After a few weeks, one glorious day, Draper tried to strike up a conversation. He had been unlocking his front door when he'd paused with his hand on the knob and called over the hedge to her.

"What are you painting?"

He'd caught her so off guard, at first she'd looked around to make sure he was actually speaking to her. Then she'd gotten so tongue-tied, she'd awkwardly merged the words *flowers* and *nothing* so that it came out as *flowthing.*

What are you painting?

Flowthing.

Draper had given her a weird squinty-eyed look, as if he'd misheard. Before she could explain herself or make a joke out of it, Draper's phone rang. He'd smiled and motioned to his cell, the international signal that he had to take the call, and disappeared inside, leaving her wishing she could fall through the porch's floorboards.

Flowthing?

How could she have said *flowthing*?

Ugh. Ugh. Ugh.

He hadn't attempted conversation since. Imagine that.

Perhaps because, ever since that mortifying day, she'd made a point of being inside when he got home. Instead of painting in the early evening, when the light was beautiful and Draper usually arrived, she'd decided to tackle her day's painting right after she got home from school, wrapping it up by four o'clock so she didn't have to face him.

It was a shame because every time she saw him, Ginny could still find something new and beautiful about his face—the light brown hair and hazel eyes, chiseled features, that brooding full bottom lip.

Draper was like a character in one of the classic books she taught in her literature classes. Mr. Darcy? Or Heathcliff?

Yes, Heathcliff!

If only she was more like Catherine Earnshaw. She could be Cathy to Draper's Heathcliff.

Her heart tripped over itself at the thought.

She loaded her brush again. With Heathcliff still on the brain, she sighed and stepped back to look at her work.

That's when the purring engine of the Porsche caught Ginny's attention. She looked up just in time to see the red sports car turning into the driveway next door, parking behind Draper's Tesla. Draper's girlfriend du jour, Ines Bartholomew, who happened to be a minor-league celebrity as a field reporter for the television show *Entertainment Right Now.* Ines slid out, catlike, from behind the wheel, fluffed her long blond hair, smoothed her black pencil skirt and walked in red-soled stilettos to Draper's front door.

The squeeze of disappointment that pinched Ginny's heart was fleeting but very real. It was ridiculous because Ines was dating him and Ginny couldn't even find the words to talk to him.

A few weeks ago, Ginny had noticed the fancy red car turn into Draper's driveway for the first time. She'd immediately recognized the beautiful woman as Ines Bartholomew. Actually, Ginny's first thought had been that the woman was a doppelgänger for Ines. Because what were the chances of someone like her being in Rambling Rose, Texas?

The minute the woman had disappeared inside Draper's house, Ginny had gone inside her own home and googled "Ines Bartholomew."

A celebrity gossip site confirmed the pair had been spotted canoodling at a charity function. It made sense. Ines was what Ginny had imagined the prototypical Draper Fortune woman would be like—movie star gorgeous, wealthy, a former Miss Texas and fourth runner-up in Miss USA.

After the initial sighting, Ginny had spied Ines's Porsche in Draper's driveway on several occasions. The car would be there when Ginny went to bed—yes, she'd checked—but it was always gone the next morning when Ginny left the house at 0 dark thirty to get her latte at Kirby's Perks before work.

This afternoon, Ginny's gaze went rogue and shot to Draper's porch just in time to see him open the door and Ines lay a big kiss on him. For a few stolen seconds, Ginny gaped at them, riveted by the sensual scene. What was it was like to be the woman who had captured Draper Fortune's heart?

The kiss gave way to an embrace. Now she had an unobstructed view of Draper's handsome face—his eyes were closed, but she knew they were an intriguing shade of hazel that made her want to pick out the various colors that made up the whole… She'd noticed his eyes the first time he'd said hello at the mailboxes.

But the memory of how she'd tripped over her words the day he'd tried to talk to her preempted the daydream.

She was cringing to herself when she realized Draper had opened those hazel eyes and was watching her. Still in Ines's arms, he raised his right hand in greeting.

White-hot pinpricks of mortification needled Ginny's body. She felt her face flame, and she was sure it was the same shade as the crimson paint on her palette.

Oh, God. Oh, God. Oh, God.

Not again.

She ducked behind her easel, hoping he'd think she'd been staring off into the middle distance and hadn't even noticed him.

A moment later, she heard the door shut.

She plunked her brushes into the mason jar filled with water and began capping her paint tubes, then tossed them into the small basket she used to transport them.

Every single time she let her guard down around Draper Fortune, she managed to make a fool out of herself.

He and his perfect girlfriend weren't even supposed to be here right now. They never arrived this early.

This is my time.

Rather than stamping her foot, she let out a quiet growl on a long, slow breath.

By the time she held the final tube of paint in her hand, her embarrassment had dulled into a muddy wash of guilt because she was using Draper and Ines as an excuse to break her promise to herself.

She hadn't finished today's painting.

Should she take her easel inside and try to salvage what was left of today's session?

She glanced down at the speckled floorboards, where the occasional errant blob of paint had landed. The porch floor could be sanded and repainted. Inside, the hardwood floors of her parents' house wouldn't be so easily fixed, which was one of the reasons she'd chosen to paint outside in the first place. It freed her from worrying about the inevitable mess that was part of the process.

Nope. Moving inside was not an option.

If she stopped before she finished this painting, she wouldn't achieve her goal for the year.

If she quit, it wouldn't be Draper's fault. It was her choice to fail at only a quarter of the way into the challenge.

What was that Eleanor Roosevelt quote about no one having the power to make you feel like an idiot... only you could do that to yourself? Or something to that tune.

She tapped her paint-smeared fingernail on the tube of cadmium yellow that she was holding in her hand, eyeing her phone, which was turned facedown on the small table.

She stared at it for a moment, as if she could will the timer to go off. When nothing happened, she sighed and picked it up.

The screen showed fourteen minutes and three seconds left on the clock.

Ginny exhaled again as she looked at her sad little painting, which amounted to nothing more than a few random strokes that hardly resembled the flowers she'd intended to paint. With the distraction of Draper and Ines pulling her out of her zone, she'd barely started.

When she was in the zone—and not distracted by the handsome guy next door and his perfect girlfriend—the time flew by. But today felt like New Year's Day, the first day of her project, all over again—the looming presence of the timer, the pressure to accomplish something, the way every little thing distracted her.

"Come on," she murmured. "You're better than that. And you're halfway through the painting." Well, according to the timer, she should be—if she hadn't been distracted by the couple next door having a life.

But really, now that Ines was here and they were inside together, the chances of them coming out again in the next—she glanced at the timer—thirteen minutes and twenty-eight seconds was slim.

Judging by that kiss, they were probably pretty busy.

"And that is none of my business."

She blinked away the thought and reset the timer for a full thirty minutes, picked up her brush and focused on the beautiful arrangement perched on the wide porch railing.

She managed to lose herself for a good twenty minutes. She knew that because when Draper's front door opened—again—her gaze darted to the timer on her phone, which she'd left faceup.

"Oh, for God's sake," she said. "I give up."

She was tempted to throw her brush across the front porch when Ines's angry voice, punctuated by a slamming door, had Ginny glancing across the hedge again.

Teetering on her stilettos, Ines gripped the handrail as she made her way down the porch steps. She looked like an angry fawn—all unsteady long legs and murderous expression. Ginny held her breath, hoping the woman didn't take a spill.

Draper opened the door and stepped onto the porch, and Ines unleashed a string of insults so unsavory that Ginny ducked behind her easel.

What fight through yonder hedgerow breaks?

Ines seemed to be the one doing all the fighting, and the words coming out of her mouth would make a biker blush.

Draper stood on the porch clutching a gold package with a red ribbon.

"Ines, wait," he said. "I don't understand."

She turned to face him. "Really, Draper? Is a box of candy the best you can do? After a month together, that's all I get? Come on, it's my birthday."

Uh-oh. Someone was in trouble.

But the way she was acting, you would've thought he had forgotten her birthday. Clearly, the chocolate was expensive. Maybe a little impersonal, but it seemed like a nice gift.

"I'm sorry you're disappointed," Draper said. "What exactly did you expect?"

Ines threw her arms in the air. "Do you really

need me to spell it out for you? If you don't know, then obviously I'm wasting my time."

Wait, were they breaking up?

Ginny knew it was wrong to eavesdrop. She should go inside and give them some privacy, especially after the earlier incident, when Draper caught her staring. But now that Ines wasn't screaming, Ginny was afraid if she moved from behind her easel, she might give herself away. So she stayed, trying to make herself as inconspicuous as possible.

"I'm sorry you feel that way," Draper said. "Will you at least take the chocolate? And let me go back inside and get the cookies that Belle baked for you."

"Don't bother." Ines spit the words like they were rotten. "In fact, you know what you can do with your box of chocolates, Forrest Gump?"

She stomped back up the porch stairs, snatched the candy from Draper's hands, turned and made her way down again, disappearing out of Ginny's view.

For a moment, Ginny wondered if, despite Ines's protests, she was going to take the chocolate with her and rage eat the entire thing, but suddenly the gold box flew over the hedge into Ginny's yard, landing in the grass with a soft thud.

The red ribbon appeared to have held the package together, because after it landed, it sat on the grass intact like a golden duck.

Was this an April Fools' joke? It was April first, after all.

The purr of the Porsche's engine and the screech

of tires as the red sports car disappeared down the street confirmed that this was no joke. Ginny's gaze moved from the candy to Draper's porch, but he wasn't there.

Poor guy.

She stood there contemplating what to do about the candy. She couldn't just leave it in the yard for racoons to devour later. Or, worse yet, to be eaten by a sweet dog, like Otis, who belonged to the Billings family two houses down.

Ginny wiped her hands on a rag and walked down to the yard to retrieve the gold box.

She'd just picked it up when Draper appeared on the sidewalk in front of her house.

"Oh!" she gasped.

Chapter Two

Draper smiled, even though he was mortified.

"The chocolate came flying over the hedge and I didn't want the Billingses' dog to get a hold of it." She gestured toward his other next-door neighbor. "You know how he gets out sometimes."

Wonderful.

If she was outside when Ines threw the box over the fence, that meant she'd likely heard the nasty lead-up to the grand finale. The whole neighborhood had probably heard the tantrum.

He'd known Ines was high-maintenance when he'd started dating her, but until this afternoon, he'd had no idea he was dealing with a diva. But Ines was the least of his concerns right now. He needed to do neighborhood damage control.

"Sorry about that." He finally found the smile that always helped him smooth over sticky situations. "Out of curiosity, how much of that did you hear?"

"Enough to know that you're better off without someone who talks to you like that." She shrugged and looked down at the box in her hands.

She was shy, this one.

Of course.

Draper didn't know why he hadn't realized that before now. Since he and his brother Beau had first moved in, she hadn't seemed very receptive when he'd tried to be neighborly. He knew that Rambling Rose natives weren't keen on the new trend of wealthy people flocking to the quiet town since his cousins had discovered it and deemed the place a diamond in the rough. When Draper and Beau had chosen to open the satellite office of their family's investment brokerage firm in Rambling Rose, they had strategically decided to move into a small house in a modest neighborhood, rather than Rambling Rose Estates, the gated community where the wealthy resided. By living simply, he and Beau had hoped they might have an easier time assimilating into the community while they grew this new branch of Fortune Investments. Of course, after Beau had gotten engaged to Sofia De Leon he'd moved out. The couple was building a new house to move into after their impending wedding.

"I'm sorry, I probably shouldn't have said that," she said. "It just slipped out. But no judgment from me."

She held out the chocolates and smiled. Or at least he hoped it was a smile. It might have been a grimace.

Draper didn't take the box. "No need to apologize. I asked, and I love your honesty."

The woman blinked.

"You do?" Now, a true smile tipped up the corners of her mouth. Draper realized she looked like a painting of the Madonna that he'd seen at the Uffizi Gallery when he was in Florence, Italy, a few years ago. She was pretty, in a wholesome way. Brown hair piled atop her head and artfully secured by a paintbrush. She didn't wear much makeup, and still her eyes were a stunning shade of blue. Another thing he couldn't believe he hadn't noticed before now.

"May I ask you a question?" he said.

"Sure."

"Is it inappropriate to give a woman chocolate as a gift?"

Those blue eyes widened. "This chocolate?"

He nodded.

"I love this chocolate," she said. "I think it's a nice gift."

"Then it's yours. Please keep it."

She shook her head and held out the box again. "Oh, no, I can't accept it."

Draper wanted to whack himself on the forehead. He must really be losing it. She'd heard him fighting with Ines, she'd seen the chocolates fly over the fence and land in her yard like yesterday's garbage. Now, here he was trying to pawn them off on her.

Smooth, Fortune. Very smooth.

"Obviously, I'm batting a thousand today," he said. "Of course, you don't want a secondhand gift, but now I'm stuck with this extremely large box of candy, and if left to my own devices, I'll probably eat the entire thing. Would you like to come in for a cup of coffee, uh…?"

And he didn't even know her name.

He laughed. "Again, I'm sorry, it's just hitting me that we've been neighbors for three months and we've never formally met. I'm Draper Fortune and I'm really messing up today, aren't I?"

She shifted the candy to the crook of her left arm and shook his outstretched hand.

"I'm Ginny Sanders." She met his gaze for the briefest moment before looking down. Twin patches of pink bloomed on her cheeks. "It's nice to officially meet you, Draper."

Her smile was sweet and her hand was soft, even if it was speckled with dried paint.

She took a step back and held out the gold box. "Here, let me give this back to you."

"I'm so sorry for the drama," he said. "I wish you'd let me make you a cup of coffee. It's the least I can offer to show you that I'm not a terrible neighbor."

Because coffee was neighborly, right?

She waved him off. "Why would I think you're a terrible neighbor? Unless you're the one who threw the chocolate in my yard. Was that you?"

Did she really think he would do something like that?

The corner of her mouth quirked into a smile.

Oh, okay! This one had a sense of humor.

"You're funny." He laughed, and when the sound tapered off, he said, "Come on, let's get some coffee."

She glanced back at her front porch. "Well, I did just finish up for the day. If making me a cup of coffee will ease your conscience, I don't see how I can refuse."

There was that smile again—mischief tempered with a dash of reserve.

"It will make me feel so much better," he said. "I can't have you thinking that I'm *that* neighbor."

"Yeah, well, we'll see," she said as they started walking toward the sidewalk. "I'll hold my opinion until I assess your coffee skills."

"Are you a coffee connoisseur?" he asked.

"Let's just say, I know my way around a coffee bar."

He answered with raised eyebrows.

"Before I started teaching full-time, I worked as a barista at Kirby's Perks for several years. That's the coffee shop downtown."

"I know the place," he said. "Man, no pressure."

He hadn't expected her to have such a dry sense of humor. That was a nice surprise. Actually, he hadn't even considered that she would have a sense of humor. Every time he'd glimpsed her on her porch painting or when they got their mail, she'd seemed like she didn't want to talk to him. Naturally, he'd concluded that she was one of the locals who was less than pleased with the Fortune invasion of Rambling Rose.

Now he realized that might not be the case.

She seemed…nice. Like a breath of fresh air compared to Ines.

She followed him onto his porch. He paused with his hand on the doorknob and nodded toward her house.

"I've noticed you painting on your porch. Are you an art teacher? I mean, you mentioned that you teach."

She grimaced. "I teach English at Rambling Rose High School. Painting is how I unwind. Sort of. Really, I'm just getting back into it."

"I'd love to see your work sometime," he said.

Her cheeks flushed again. "It's just stuff I do for myself. I'd never considered showing it to anyone else."

"Why not?" he said. "I thought every artist's goal was to sell their work."

He knew that wasn't always the case, but it was fun sparring with her. He wanted to see her reaction.

She shook her head and looked equal parts perplexed and horrified.

"No, that's not *every* artist's goal. Sometimes it's enough just to paint."

He pushed open the door and motioned for her

to enter first. "Do you paint landscapes, portraits or abstracts?"

She stopped in the living room and turned to face him.

"None of the above. I paint still life. Or at least that's what I'm doing right now. Actually, you might call it abstract still life." She told him of her goal to finish a painting every day for a year.

"That's ambitious."

She shrugged, as if dismissing the conversation. Her gaze darted around the room.

"It's funny, this place looks exactly the same as when the Dobsons lived here," she said.

"Technically, they do still live here. My brother and I rented the place while they're traveling. They were nice to let it fully furnished. Since Beau moved out, and it's just me, there was no need to invest in furniture. Especially since the Dobsons will be back eventually and I'll have to move out."

"Where will you move?" she asked.

"That's a good question."

He'd sort it out by the time the Dobsons returned. Now that he and Beau had made the new branch a success, he would buy a place, but the jury was still out as to whether he would stay local or move to Austin, where things were a bit livelier than Rambling Rose. Of course, his first choice would be to get a nice promotion and move back to the home office in New Orleans. But right now, it was all up in the air.

"If you were a barista, I'm guessing you don't mind your coffee strong?"

"As long as it's flavorful."

"Have a seat." He motioned to the kitchen table and prepped the pot. "How about a cappuccino?"

"That sounds great."

He took pride in grinding the beans, knowing she would appreciate that touch. Once he'd readied the pot and placed it on the gas burner, he set out two small plates, opened the box of candy and the plastic container of snickerdoodle cookies his sister, Belle, had made for Ines. The very ones that had made the woman sprout virtual horns and fangs.

"These look delicious." Ginny bit into a cookie and closed her eyes as she chewed. "*Umm.* Cookies are my weakness. Actually, I can't resist sweets in general."

"My sister is quite the baker."

"I'll say. She should talk to my friend, Kirby Harris. She owns Kirby's Perks. I'll bet she'd buy these for her customers."

"I think Belle's baking obsession is more of a hobby, but she does enjoy baking for the people she cares about. I'm glad you're enjoying them because she would be crushed if she knew how Ines had reacted when I gave them to her. I mean, I guess you heard the fight."

Ginny shrugged.

Shaking his head, he chose a piece of chocolate

and held out the box to Ginny. She took one out and set it on her plate. "I'd better pace myself."

It was nice to meet a woman with an appetite. Most of the women he knew seemed to subsist on lettuce and champagne. Ines usually picked at her food and left most of it on her plate. He understood that television was a cutthroat business and he appreciated the hard work and sacrifice it took for Ines to maintain her figure, but lately, he realized she took it to an unhealthy extreme.

It didn't have to be that way. Curves were sexy.

Take Ginny, for example. She wasn't afraid to indulge. She wasn't skinny…but her curves were nice. Draper looked up to steal a glance. She was looking at him.

He smiled, relieved he hadn't allowed his gaze to meander. To remove himself from further temptation, he went to the stove to pour the espresso for their cappuccinos.

"Not to be nosy," she said. "But why did your girlfriend take issue with the cookies and chocolate?"

Draper shook his head. "She's not my girlfriend."

Even the thought of being tied down to Ines—or anyone, for that matter—made him feel itchy and claustrophobic. What was the point? He loved the ladies. Emphasis on the plural. He wasn't a one-woman, in-it-for-the-long-haul, ball and chain kind of guy. Nope, committing to one woman *'til death do us part* was not his idea of a good time.

"Oh, sorry. I thought she was..." Ginny waved her hand as if she could clear away the words.

As Draper frothed the milk, he weighed his words. "It's complicated and there are a lot of things that I shouldn't go into, but since you had a front row seat for today's spectacle, I feel like I owe you an explanation."

He poured the liquid into cups and carefully distributed the foamed milk on top. "Today is her birthday, and I feel bad that she got upset, but she was in a mood when she got here. When I gave her the cookies Belle baked for her, she called the gesture *quaint*—can you believe she said that? My sister took time out of her life to bake for Ines and that's the thanks she gets?"

Ginny swiped at the corners of her mouth, returned the rest of the uneaten cookie to her plate and put her hands in her lap.

"Then I made the mistake of giving her the candy. After seeing her reaction to Belle's cookies, I should've known better. Long story short, she was disappointed by what she perceived to be an impersonal gift. That led to a very brief where-is-this-relationship-going talk. Since she asked, I had no choice but to clarify that while I enjoy spending time with her, I am not the marrying type. If that's what she was looking for, she was barking up the wrong tree. With that, she stomped out. I think you heard the rest."

Ginny nodded and pulled a one-shoulder shrug.

The way the late afternoon light was streaming in through the kitchen window highlighted a cute dusting of freckles across the bridge of her nose. How had he not noticed those before now? Then again, he'd never been into the girl next door type. So it really didn't matter.

He cleared his throat. "Anyway, we were supposed to go out to dinner tonight. What Ines didn't know is I had another gift for her, a gold bracelet that I'd planned to give her at dinner."

He set the cups on the table and took a seat next to Ginny.

"As far as I'm concerned, her reaction to the *quaint* birthday presents revealed her true nature. If she's only in it for the expensive gifts, then it's best that we parted ways."

Silence seemed to hang in the air like a bad smell that Ginny was too polite to mention.

He'd probably said too much, but it was already out in the open.

"What?" he said. "Am I wrong?"

She grimaced. "Do you want me to tell you what I think you want to hear or do you want me to be real with you?"

"Give it to me straight, please," he said, steeling himself.

"She's not your girlfriend, but you bought her an expensive bracelet?"

"Yes, I mean, it's no big deal. The reality is, it's the kind of gift a woman like Ines expects."

"But you just said you were letting her go because she was only in it for the gifts. If you knew she was expecting something expensive and you bought her something expensive, it seems like you might be feeding that monster. Or at the very least, sending mixed signals."

Ginny feared she'd said too much, but the horse was already out of the proverbial barn.

She felt both flattered and a little depressed over the way Draper had opened up to her. Flattered that he was interested in her point of view, but depressed because if a stunner like Ines couldn't grab hold of Draper's heart, what possible chance did she have with him?

As if it was even a possibility. Less than a half-hour ago she'd been hiding behind her easel praying he wouldn't notice her. Until Ines had chucked the chocolates, Ginny had never dreamed she'd be having a coherent conversation with the guy, much less sitting in his kitchen having coffee with him.

She gave herself a mental shake. She might have a little crush on him, but that was as far as it would go.

"Hey, listen, I'm sorry. I didn't ask you over for coffee to dump all my problems on you. I just wanted you to know that in the future my dates won't make a habit of throwing things in your yard."

"It's not a problem," she said. "Really."

He laughed. The hollow sound seemed to echo in the ensuing silence. She racked her brain, trying to think of something to say to divert the conversation away from the awkwardness looming between them.

His phone rang and he pulled it from his back pocket.

"I'm sorry," he said. "I need to take this."

"I should go," she said at the same time he said, "This is Draper Fortune."

He motioned to her to stay and mouthed, "I'll be right back," before he left the room.

It was probably Ines calling to say she'd made a big mistake and wanted to come back for her cookies and candy and any other sweets Draper might have in store for her.

Or maybe it wasn't.

Either way it was none of her business. She had been unwittingly inserted into the middle of the situation. If anything good had come from it, at least she'd had a chance to prove to him—and herself—that she wasn't an idiot who blurted out nonsensical words every time he attempted conversation. She could be her normal self around him. Then again, she'd also verified he was at once human, yet somehow still untouchable.

At least now they were on speaking terms.

Maybe in the future she'd say hello to him.

Maybe.

Yeah, and then what? He'd go back to his high-maintenance women and she'd go back to living vicariously from the safety of her front porch.

She stood so she'd be ready to leave when Draper

returned. As she waited, she left the kitchen and glanced around the Dobsons' living room. Ginny had gone to school with Terry Dobson, who was a year younger. They used to be friendly when they were in middle school, but had drifted into different circles when they were in high school. Ginny hadn't seen the inside of this house in ages, but the place looked exactly as she remembered.

Same overstuffed circa-1990s brown leather couch. Same brown-and-orange-plaid easy chairs. Same wood-and-glass coffee table. Somehow she'd expected the place to look fancier after the Fortune brothers had graced the place with their presence.

A pink throw that was draped over the arm of the couch caught her eye because it seemed out of place.

Actually, the pink throw looked like a baby blanket.

Maybe it was something Mrs. Dobson had left? Had Terry had a baby? Ginny hadn't even heard that she'd gotten married. Not that she had to be married, but…

She walked over to the couch, picked up the blanket and held it up.

It sure was a pink baby blanket, the soft flannel variety, and it was embroidered with an *F.*

*F…*as in Fortune?

But which Fortune? Surely, Draper wasn't a father? Or was he?

Maybe it was baby gift for one of the five Fortune couples who had gotten married on New Year's Eve.

Everything about that wedding seemed romantic. It would stand to reason that one of the lucky couples would be blessed with a baby so soon after the wedding. That would be the perfect ending—or next chapter—to a perfect fairy tale.

It would be wonderful to have a family. She adored children. That was one of the reasons she had gone in to teaching. Yet, as much as she wanted a family of her own, she had a lot of stuff she needed to sort through before she could be a good mother…or wife.

"Sorry about that," Draper said.

Ginny froze at the sound of his voice. Her mind raced as she looked for a reasonable explanation of why she was in the living room holding the blanket. She was cold. Yeah, right. She was curious. True, but she would look like an insufferable snoop. She hadn't meant to be, but…

"Pink isn't exactly your color," she said as she folded the blanket. Making sure the embroidered *F* was front and center, she returned it to the arm of the couch where she'd found it.

"I know, right?" Draper said. "I wouldn't have chosen that color. I'm more of a mint-green man, myself. But the blanket doesn't belong to me. It arrived last month addressed to my brother Beau."

Ginny's eyes widened. She knew that Beau had recently gotten engaged. Were he and Sofia expecting?

Draper must've read her thoughts because he shook his head.

"We have no idea where it came from or who sent it," he said. "It's pretty weird, but it's also kind of funny. So we figured that it's someone's idea of a joke, and we've been passing it back and forth like a hot potato, pawning it off on each other since Beau moved out. He was over here yesterday. I hadn't realized he'd left it, even though it's right there in front of my face. Let's sit down."

He gestured to the couch.

Awareness needled Ginny and she felt her face go warm again as she realized she and Draper were alone in the house. Sitting in the kitchen having coffee was one thing, but —

"I really should go," she said. "You probably have a million things to do."

"Actually, I don't. My evening is unexpectedly free."

Well, that answered the question about whether Ines had called to say she had changed her mind and was on her way back.

Draper sat down on the sofa and Ginny followed suit, perching on the edge of the cushion, leaving a respectable amount of space between the two of them.

Her heart kicked against her rib cage, beating so fast she was afraid he might hear it. That or the sound of her breathing, which suddenly seemed so thick she could barely get any air in her lungs.

She'd missed her opportunity for an easy exit before she sat down next to him, and now she was teetering on the edge of an anxiety attack. She knew better than to put herself in a position like this. It had been more than a decade since…that night, but the emotional scars still burned.

Why wasn't she just straightforward with him? Why didn't she say she was the one who had a lot to do? Why? Because this was Draper *Fricking* Fortune. She would probably never have the opportunity to sit next to him on a couch again. But being alone with any man and sitting next to him on a couch was all it took to—

"…and so now I have an extra ticket and it's tomorrow," he said. "I know it's short notice, but what do you think?"

Wait. What?

OMG, had he been talking to her this whole time? She'd been so deep in her head that she'd missed the entire context of what he was saying.

He was smiling at her. Looking hopeful and expectant. He was waiting for her to answer. But she had no idea what to say because she hadn't heard a word he'd said. Should she just admit that she'd zoned out and ask him to repeat himself?

She tried to will the words from her brain to her tongue, but they got caught in the massive cringe that was constricting her throat.

His smile faltered and he made a disappointed sound. "It's last-minute. So if you already have plans, I understand. I just thought I'd ask, but obviously a beautiful woman like you has her choice of things to do on a Saturday night."

A beautiful woman like you.

Me?

Draper Fortune had called her beautiful.

And had he just asked her out?

Say something, dammit!

"Yes," she murmured.

"Yes?" he asked. "'Yes,' you'll go, or 'yes,' you're booked?"

His smile was dazzling, but the hint of vulnerability in his hazel eyes tugged at her heart. It seemed as if it really mattered to him whether she said yes or no.

Little did he know that even if she had a date with Chris Hemsworth, she'd break it and go…wherever it was that Draper wanted to take her.

But this wasn't really a *date*, she reminded herself, because he'd just broken up with Ines, who he'd sworn wasn't his girlfriend, but who probably was his original date…

Stop overthinking it.

"I'd love to join you."

Even if I'll simply be a place filler and I have no idea where I'm going...

It would be another chance to see him.

"Fantastic." His smile seemed genuine.

She really should ask for specifics, even if it made her look like a flake.

She stood already second guessing herself. Was going somewhere with him a good idea when sitting next to him on a couch had nearly sent her into a panic attack?

She steeled herself to ask where they were going, but her mouth wouldn't cooperate. All she could think of was *flowthing*, but she managed to spit out a few words. "I really should go."

"Of course." Draper stood, too, looking pleased. "I'll pick you up at six o'clock tomorrow evening. Dress to impress."

Chapter Three

When Ginny got home she immediately called her best friend, Kirby Harris.

"You won't believe what's happened this afternoon," she said and filled in Kirby on everything from the argument she'd overheard, to the box of chocolate sailing over the hedge, to the coffee with Draper and ending with the near panic attack that made her zone out and miss the gist of his question.

"Leave it to me," Ginny said. "For months I've fantasized about Draper Fortune asking me out—never really believing it would happen, of course—and when that magic moment arrives, I'm so in my head I miss it."

"Okay, you need to reframe your thinking," Kirby

said. "Is the glass half-empty or half-full? If I were you, I'd forget the nonsense and anticipate the fine wine that is Draper Fortune."

One of the things that Ginny loved best about her friend was how she was always real with her, no matter how difficult the subject. Kirby had a gentle straightforward way that got to the heart of the matter.

"I know, but what the heck does 'dress to impress' even mean?" Ginny lamented as the reality of the situation sank in. "Do you think it's too late to bow out?"

"You are not canceling on him," Kirby said. "I've got you. So stop worrying. Come over tomorrow morning and we'll figure it out, okay?"

Ginny tossed and turned all night, slipping in and out of dreams. In one, Ines showed up at the event and accused Ginny of stealing Draper. In another, she accused Ginny of stealing her dress, and when Ginny had looked down at her own body she'd been horrified to realize that she was wearing nothing at all…and Ines was standing there, her arm linked through Draper's, holding up the beaded gown. Everyone in the room laughed and pointed at Ginny as she tried to cover herself and make her escape.

She bolted upright in bed, vowing to cancel as soon as the hour was decent enough for her to go over and knock on Draper's door.

She imagined his face since she wouldn't be leaving him much time to find a replacement…date.

She drifted off to sleep again, fighting the dread of breaking that news. Finally when her alarm went off at seven o'clock, she felt more refreshed than she thought she would. She redoubled her resolve and decided she was going to do this.

She was going out with Draper Fortune tonight.

But what was she going to wear?

He'd said to dress to impress.

Her work clothes hardly fit the bill. It wasn't in her budget to buy something new, and even if it was, what should she buy? Formal wear? A cocktail dress? Something chic and sleek like Ines would wear?

She wasn't like Ines or any of the other women she'd seen Draper with since he'd moved in next door.

She took a slow, deep breath and gave herself a pep talk. Under normal circumstances, she was fine just the way she was—actually, when it came down to it, she was pretty okay with herself…when she kept to herself. The problem was putting herself out there like this made her feel unsure. But putting herself out there in a world that wasn't her own didn't change who she was. She would be okay no matter what happened.

Actually, maybe getting a dose of Draper Fortune and his world would help her get over her crush, or at least put it into perspective.

He was just a man, who put on his pants like every other man in the world. And took off those pants like other men…the thought hit her like a punch in the gut, but she took a deep breath and reminded herself not every man was out to take advantage of women.

And she wasn't the trusting naive girl she'd been all those years ago.

She needed to keep her wits about her and stay grounded in reality. The Draper Fortune who lived in her head wasn't necessarily the Draper Fortune who walked this earth. Based on what he'd said, he'd been candid with Ines about the fact that he wasn't interested in a serious relationship. Even if he might be prone to sending mixed signals, he seemed like a good person. Like a man who would never hurt a woman, emotionally or physically.

Even so, she would be on her guard. Just as she had been with the handful of men she'd been out with over the last decade.

The ring of her cell phone startled Ginny back to earth. When she glanced at the screen, a photo of Kirby's beautiful face smiled back at her, and Ginny couldn't suppress a smile of her own.

"Good morning," Ginny said.

"Yes, it is a good morning," Kirby said. "Want to come for breakfast? The girls and I are making blueberry pancakes."

Ginny's stomach growled. "Yes, please. I'm starving and I hadn't even realized it until you said pancakes. I'm leaving to come over now."

Kirby was one of the strongest women that Ginny had ever met. Three years ago, she had lost her husband, Will, to an aggressive form of cancer. Since then, she had run her coffeehouse, Kirby's Perks, and raised her daughters, seven-year-old Violet and five-year-old Lily, mostly on her own.

The minute Ginny pulled into Kirby's driveway, Violet and Lily ran out to greet her. She opened the car door and spread her arms wide, and the girls smothered her with hugs and giggles.

"Did you bring the art supplies?" Violet asked.

"You know I did," Ginny said.

"What did you bring?" asked Lily, jumping up and down.

Ginny reached over and grabbed the handles of one of the two canvas bags on the passenger seat.

"Look in here and see if there's anything you like."

Violet immediately took possession.

"I get to look first because I'm the oldest," she said.

Lily crossed her arms, tucked her chin and stuck out her bottom lip.

Anticipating the sibling rivalry, Ginny had brought two bags.

"I just happen to have another bag of goodies for Miss Lily." Ginny reached over and pulled out an identical bag. "You look through this one. I'll bet you'll find some fun stuff."

The girls thanked her with more hugs.

Right after the New Year, Ginny had partnered with the school's art teacher and started an art club at the high school. When she ordered supplies with the money the PTA provided, the various vendors always sent an abundance of samples. In the most recent order, they'd included tote bags for the kids. Ginny had had more than enough for the students and had been delighted to bring bags of sketching pencils, crayons, watercolors, brushes and paper for Violet and Lily.

"After we eat breakfast, your mom is going to help me with something," she said. "While we're busy, will you each draw or paint me a picture?"

The girls nodded enthusiastically.

Kirby opened the front door. Dressed in jeans and a yellow blouse, her naturally wavy black hair was pulled off her pretty face by a headband and hung down her back. "Excuse me, girls, I thought you had volunteered to make the pancakes? Or should Ginny and I do it? It's kind of fun, so we wouldn't mind."

"We want to do it!" the girls said in unison as they ran with their bags toward the front door. They disappeared inside before Ginny made it to the porch.

"See what I did there?" Kirby smiled.

"That was masterful," Ginny said. "I wish that approach worked on high schoolers."

Kirby sighed. "As fast as they're growing up, they'll be in high school before I'm ready."

"That's why we need to enjoy every minute while they're young," Ginny said.

For a split second, a cloud of sadness flashed in Kirby's eyes. "No one knows that better than I do."

Ginny knew Kirby was thinking of Will, but

never one to wallow, her friend nodded and the sparkle returned to her pretty brown eyes.

"I hope you don't mind free-form pancakes," she said. "The girls are just learning."

"The free-form ones taste the most delicious," Ginny said.

"What was in those bags you gave them?"

"Just some extra art supplies that I got from the art club," she said. "I must warn you, I gave them paint. So you might want to set some ground rules."

Kirby smiled her appreciation. "You spoil them."

"Every chance I get," Ginny said. "If we have time today, I'll give them an art lesson."

Kirby looked at her watch. "I don't know if we will. Our priority is to get you ready for this date."

Ginny groaned. "Or I could stay here with them instead of going out."

Kirby elbowed Ginny playfully as she stepped through the front door and into Kirby's living room. "Confidence, Ginny. By the time I'm finished with you, Draper Fortune won't know what hit him."

"Yeah, we'll see."

The fact that she was seeing Draper tonight kept hitting Ginny in waves. Sometimes the waves were small and manageable, other times, like now, they smacked into her and threatened to knock her down. "So does this mean I get to help you get ready for a date in the near future? It's the least I can do."

Kirby frowned. "One day at a time. Or should I say, one date at a time? Let's get you situated and then we'll think about me. But first, let's eat some pancakes."

Kirby smiled, but Ginny saw the flicker of pain in Kirby's eyes.

At thirty-four, her friend was too young to put herself on a shelf. Even if Kirby's late husband had been her soul mate, Ginny knew that he would want her to find love again and be happy.

Ginny had tried to entice Kirby to get out more by offering to babysit. She had said over and over the best tribute Kirby could pay Will was to find love again, because that meant that the life she'd known with him was happy and she wanted to find that feeling again. Kirby insisted that because life with Will had been so happy, she would be hard-pressed to find someone who made her feel that way again. Therefore, by going out she was setting herself up for disappointment.

She maintained that love was a once-in-a-lifetime treasure and she had been blessed having known such a great love even if it had been short-lived.

That always left Ginny at a loss for words because she had never known romantic love as deep as what Kirby and Will had shared.

Ginny had been fortunate to have a close family—parents who adored her and would do anything for her and protective older brothers who looked out for her. But true love in the romantic sense seemed to elude her.

She'd dated Bobby Hicks all through high school,

but when she'd gotten accepted to the University of Texas at Austin and he hadn't, they had decided to take a break, which ended when Bobby got Patty Tobias pregnant and the two got married.

Then, of course, what happened in college had not only made Ginny give up art, but it also made her question if she even wanted to date.

"I want to pour the pancake batter," Lily cried as Ginny and Kirby walked into the kitchen.

"No! You're supposed to put the blueberries on the pancake after I pour it into the skillet," Violet yelled back.

"Girls, why don't you just mix the berries into the batter?" Ginny suggested. "Wouldn't that be easier?"

"If you do it that way," said Kirby, "the pancakes turn purple."

"What's wrong with purple pancakes?" Ginny asked.

Without hesitating, Kirby picked up the carton of blueberries and dumped them into the batter. As she stirred, the residual juice bled into the batter like watercolor paint on a piece of primed cold-press paper. "Sometimes you need to step outside your comfort zone, right, Ginny?" She gave her friend a knowing look. "I think purple pancakes are exactly what this day calls for."

About an hour later, after they'd eaten breakfast and the girls were painting at the kitchen table, Ginny and Kirby retreated to Kirby's bedroom, where she began pulling dresses from her closet.

"Did you get a chance to ask Draper where you're going?" she asked as she regarded a silky blue jumpsuit, shook her head and returned it to the closet.

"No," Ginny said. "I didn't want to knock on his door so early on a Saturday morning."

When Kirby shot her a look, Ginny covered her face with her hands. "It's embarrassing. It all happened so fast and I was overwhelmed. All I know is he has an extra ticket to wherever we're going and I should dress to impress."

"So I take it you're not going to a movie," Kirby said.

"Not unless it's an extra fancy movie."

"Why didn't you just ask him to tell you more about the event?"

"Don't judge," Ginny wailed. "I already feel like an idiot. You know how I am. I thought of exactly what I should've done a couple of hours later, but by that time it was too late to ask for more information."

"I'm not judging you," Kirby said. "You know I'd never do that. Wait—I know what you need to wear."

She pulled a dress from her closet. "You can never go wrong with a little black dress and this one is perfect. Understated enough to be classy, but sexy enough to knock the socks off of Mr. Draper Fortune. Go try it on. With these."

Kirby pulled a pair of strappy black sandals from the top shelf of her closet.

Ginny pressed her lips together, trying to stave off the dubious feeling that was trying to bully its way to the surface. Kirby was tall and thin. In fact, she was a good five inches taller than Ginny. She was gorgeous with a natural grace and elegance about her that would allow her to carry off a look like this.

Ginny started to protest but stopped. Kirby was dedicating a rare Saturday morning off to her, trying to help her get ready for her big date. The least Ginny could do was try on the outfit. After all, anything in Kirby's wardrobe would be better than what Ginny had at home in her closet.

She took the dress and shoes into the bathroom, fighting the sinking feeling that not only would the dress not fit, but that she was also in way over her head when it came to Draper Fortune.

"Come out and model it for me after you have it on," Kirby said through the bathroom door.

As she took the dress off the hanger, Ginny saw that the garment still had the tags on it.

"Hey, Kirbs," Ginny called as she opened the door. "This dress is beautiful, but you haven't even worn it."

Kirby nodded and her lips disappeared into a pensive thin line.

"I just… I never got the opportunity." Kirby gave a one-shoulder shrug and tried to smile, but it didn't reach her brown eyes.

Ginny knew there was more to the story.

While her friend always looked gorgeous, even when she was behind the coffee bar wearing jeans and her apron, Ginny knew Kirby well enough to know she wasn't the type who bought expensive dresses just to hang in her closet…especially when she still wasn't dating.

"Why not?" Ginny persisted.

Kirby's eyes pooled and she tried to wave away the question.

"Kirby? Please tell me."

The woman drew in a deep breath and closed her eyes as she exhaled slowly.

Finally, she said, "I got this dress right before Will got sick. It was for our anniversary, but his diagnosis came back with the worst possible news before we could celebrate. Then he just kept getting sicker and sicker. Two months later, he was gone—" Her voice caught on the last word.

Ginny put her arms around her friend, and they stayed like that until Kirby gathered herself and pulled away, swiping at the few tears that clung to her long, dark lashes.

"I'm sorry, Kirbs. This is too upsetting for you."

"No, really, it's not. It's just that I hadn't even thought about that dress in such a long time. It's bringing up a lot of feelings."

"Of course, it is."

"One of the most unexpected feelings is the realization that even though I still miss Will, time has lessened the pain."

"Maybe you're ready to dip your toe into the dating pool?"

Kirby shook her head. "You know I don't have time to date."

"You make time for what's important," Ginny said. "And you know you always have a babysitter. I'll keep the girls anytime you want."

Kirby started to say something but stopped.

"What?" Ginny asked.

Again, Kirby shook her head and turned her attention to her closet. She pulled a pretty black beaded clutch from the top shelf and handed it to Ginny. "You'll need this, too."

"Thank you, but you changed the subject. You know Will would want you to be happy."

"I am happy. Or happier. I have my girls, my family, good friends, my business. My life is full." She shrugged. "What's the point of dating when I don't know if I'll ever be able to fall in love again? But, hey, today is about you. Go try on the dress."

Ginny hesitated, glancing down at the dress and clutch in her hands.

Will was an exceptional man and it would take someone spectacular to capture Kirby's heart. Even so, Ginny wasn't giving up. Kirby lending her the dress was a big deal and it seemed to be a step toward healing, but maybe she needed a few more baby steps before she could run into the arms of a new love.

"Am I going to have to dress you myself, like I do the girls on the mornings when they're lollygagging and making me late?"

They both laughed at the absurdity. Then Ginny sobered.

"Are you sure?" She held up the dress. "This feels like a big deal."

"It is a big deal," Kirby said. "I don't lend my clothes to everyone, you know?"

They laughed again.

"No, seriously," Kirby said. "The best thing you could do for me would be to wear this beautiful dress on your date tonight—and make that man fall in love with you."

Well, that was about as likely to happen as it was that she would be able to stuff her body into this little number.

Still, Ginny smiled and disappeared inside the bathroom again.

When the silky fabric fell into place on Ginny's body and she realized she could zip it up with ease, her pulse quickened.

The figure-skimming material had a bit of give and somehow adjusted itself to Ginny's curves, pulling up the hem of the A-line skirt so that it hit right at her knees. In fact…

"This could work."

No, more than that. It was perfect.

She slipped on the sandals and then turned this way and that in front of the full-length mirror on the bathroom door.

Yes, this could definitely work. It was breathtaking. Kirby was right; the off the shoulder dress had a fitted bodice that showcased Ginny's décolletage perfectly. It was equal parts classy and understatedly sexy.

Maybe this was a good sign that everything would be okay tonight.

Well, at least until the stroke of midnight, when her coach turned into a pumpkin, because right now, she felt like Cinderella getting ready for the ball.

Kirby knocked. "How are you doing in there? Do you need me to zip you up?"

Ginny opened the bathroom door and stepped out.

Kirby gasped and her hand fluttered to her mouth.

"I knew it," she said. "I knew it would look perfect on you. Come over here."

Kirby brushed past her into the bathroom. Ginny followed her to the vanity area. With a renewed look of determination, Kirby grabbed a brush from a drawer and swept Ginny's hair into a makeshift French twist, which she fastened into place with a few pins.

"I'll be right back."

A moment later, Kirby returned with two small boxes. The first one held a creamy pearl necklace, which she looped around Ginny's neck. The second one held a pair of delicate pearl-and-diamond earrings.

"Audrey Hepburn, eat your heart out," Kirby said as she stepped back to admire her work. "All you need is a little bit of makeup and some nail polish on your fingers and—" She glanced down at Ginny's feet and grimaced. "Please, go get a pedicure. After that, you'll be ready for the ball, Cinderella. Or wherever it is that Prince Charming is taking you."

They were quiet for a moment as they both studied Ginny's reflection in the mirror.

"You really do look stunning," Kirby said. "But the most important thing is how do you feel?"

Ginny stared at herself, hardly believing the transformation.

"I feel great, but are you absolutely sure this is okay? It's not too late to change your mind about the dress."

Kirby nodded resolutely and then smiled her benevolent smile. She always put the people she cared about first.

Ginny turned to Kirby. "Thank you." The words were a whisper because she was afraid if she said anything more, she would lose her composure, and Kirby would hate that. She turned back to the mirror and examined herself again, daring to let herself feel the slightest twinge of excitement for the night ahead.

Chapter Four

With her dress, shoes and accessories in place, Ginny ran home and made quick work of completing her daily painting. After that, she went to the Live and Let Dye salon, where they'd been gracious enough to squeeze her in for a French manicure and pedicure with classic red polish. Since she wasn't among the regulars, she had to endure a bit of grilling about what occasion had brought her in today.

"So what's going on, hon?" asked Honey, as she drew water into the tub of the pedicure chair.

"Nothing special. I just thought I'd treat myself."

The salon's front door opened and the chime sounded, a snippet of the salon's namesake tune, "Live and Let Die."

Honey quirked a questioning eyebrow at Ginny before she turned to deal with the woman who had just walked in. When she returned to Ginny, she said, "I'm going to pour myself a coffee. Want one?"

"Thank you, Honey. That sounds great."

Ginny didn't want the coffee as much as she wanted the break in conversation, a chance to steer Honey away from why she had all but begged them to work her in on a busy Saturday morning when everyone knew manis and pedis weren't her usual thing.

That was because the acrylic paint she used on canvases ruined any manicure. In fact, today's magic would be undone tomorrow when Ginny returned to her easel.

She stared down at her hands—the short nails, the ragged cuticles, the faint hint of paint stain on her knuckles.

She could always wear gloves.

Yes. That's what she'd do. She'd wear gloves. Make it last longer.

She sank back into the leatherette chair and closed her eyes as she enjoyed the feeling of the warm water splashing over her feet. Closing her eyes might also help her not get snared in the salon's gossip trap.

The moment she'd secured the appointment, she had promised herself to keep mum about tonight's date—or whatever it was—with Draper. The handful of single Fortune men who had moved to the area were hot commodities in town. When any one of them had a date, it stirred up awe and envy among Rambling Rose's eligible women and romantics.

If word got out, it would cause a commotion because Ginny was one of the least likely candidates to catch a Fortune—and that wasn't negative self-talk. The proof was in the history.

Fortune men went for women like Sofia De Leon, a Tejano businesswoman who was as brilliant as she was beautiful. No one had been surprised when all-work-and-no-play Beau Fortune had fallen hard for her and proposed.

Of course, there were Wiley Fortune and Grace Williams, Kane Fortune and Layla McCarthy, and Brady Fortune and Harper Radcliffe, all of whom had said "I do" at the infamous Fortune quintet wedding on New Year's Eve, which had inflamed Ginny's discontent and opened her to welcoming change into her life.

Maybe her plan was working. At least she had been painting every day and she had finally gone from daydreaming about Draper Fortune to—to talking to him.

That's what they were doing. They were *talking*... as the kids in her classes would say when pressed about the nature of their relationship with someone they'd been hanging out with.

Kids these days didn't date. They *talked*.

Ginny pressed the button to activate the massage function on the chair and imagined the scene that would ensue if she announced to everyone in the salon that "Draper Fortune and I are talking"...much less if she said they had a date tonight.

"What are you smiling about?" Honey asked as she returned with two steaming cups of coffee.

"Just relaxing and enjoying myself," Ginny said.

Honey took her place on the stool in front of the soaking tub and lifted one of Ginny's feet out of the water, then eyed her neglected foot. "Well, good for you, hon. I'm glad to see you're finally taking an interest in self-care."

Unsure of what to say at that little dig, Ginny changed the subject. "I'd hoped to treat Kirby to a mani-pedi today because she had the day off, but we couldn't align our schedules."

It was true, Ginny had invited Kirby along as a thank-you for all she'd done, but Honey only had room to work in one appointment, saying it would be tight at that. Kirby had waved her off, claiming she needed to stop by the coffeehouse to check on inventory after she dropped off Violet and Lily for playdates.

"Next time plan ahead and we'll get the two of you in together," Honey said.

The salon was small and only allowed enough room for one pedicure chair and one manicure station behind the hairstylists' chairs. If they'd come in together, one would get fingernails done while the other was having a pedi, but that would be okay.

Honey didn't get a chance to press Ginny for her post-pedi plans because Jewel Abernathy, who looked like she was wired for television reception with all the foils on her head, piped up and said, "Hey, did y'all hear that one of those Fortune boys is dating that little girl from that celebrity gossip show? Oh, what's her name? Enid something or the other?"

Ginny had to bite her lip to keep from saying, "Her name is Ines. Ines Bartholomew. And, no, Draper is not seeing her. Not anymore."

They didn't even realize that the Fortune *boy* in question lived right next door to her. If they were aware, they'd be pumping her for details. As far as they were concerned, she was quiet Ginny Sanders, the schoolteacher who rarely dated and mostly kept to herself. Actually, they probably didn't even give her that much thought because she had never given them anything to talk about.

All the more reason to keep it that way and not offer a word about her night out with Draper. That wasn't difficult because she couldn't get a word in edgewise after the Fortune talk began.

Ginny had fun relaying the salon buzz to Kirby when they met at her house later that afternoon. Kirby had insisted that Ginny come by so she could do her hair and makeup.

After the day of glam, Ginny got home around four thirty. The only thing she had left to do was slip into the dress and shoes…and wait for Draper to ring the bell at six o'clock.

By five thirty, she'd touched up her lipstick,

smoothed her hair and made sure she had everything she needed in the black beaded clutch that Kirby had loaned her. She'd forced herself to wait until five forty-five to get dressed because she didn't want to sit and wrinkle the dress, but that only took a moment. There was plenty of time for the nerves to swarm and buzz in her stomach.

Ready to go, she walked downstairs at five minutes until six. That's when her brother Jerry, whom she'd casually told she had "plans with a friend," walked in the kitchen door, an hour earlier than he was supposed to be home.

He let loose a long whistle. "Excuse me, I was looking for my sister. What have you done with her?"

"Very funny, Jer."

"I have to say, you clean up nicely. I haven't seen you this gussied up since your senior prom. Are you chaperoning a dance I don't know about?"

For school events where the kids wore formal wear or cocktail dresses, Ginny always wore a nice dress, but nothing this fancy. She figured it was the kids' night to shine and she had no business getting "gussied up," as Jerry had teased. Not to mention she didn't have anything much swankier than a regular dress.

"Wait a minute," Jerry said. "You said you were going out with a friend. I assumed you and Kirby were going to a movie or book club or something. Who is this *friend*?"

"Just a—a friend," she said. "Mind your own business. Don't you have your own plans you need to start getting ready for?"

"Nothing that can't wait. I was just meeting Josh Fortune for a beer."

Josh had moved to town not long after the big New Year's Eve Fortune wedding. He and Jerry had met when Josh was doing some repair work on the ranch where Jerry worked. The two had become fast friends.

Of course, since Josh was a Fortune, it meant that he and Draper were related even though they were as different as night and day. Josh was laidback and casual. Draper was all business and…gorgeous.

She placed her hand on her stomach to quell the sudden flutter.

That's when she realized Jerry was squinting at her… scrutinizing her.

"Someone has a date."

"Well, I'm sure *someone* out there in the world does. Probably a lot of someones, for that matter."

She and Jerry were close. Besides Kirby, Jerry was the only other person in whom she'd confided about her ennui and her resolution to reshape her life. He was as much a friend as a brother. So why not tell him she was going out with Draper tonight?

She was ready to confess when the doorbell rang.

Jerry smiled. "I'll get that."

"No, Jerry, let me."

"Just be cool," he said. "You don't want to look too eager. In fact, stay in here and make him wait a minute or two, then make an entrance. It will give me a chance to ask his intentions."

"Jerry, don't embarrass me."

His playful expression softened. "I would never embarrass you. I promise."

She glanced at the living room clock. Six o'clock sharp. She had to hand it to Draper—the man was punctual. It was a quality that Ginny admired.

She counted to thirty before she walked down the hall toward the front door, doing her very best to channel her inner Audrey Hepburn.

It must've worked because Draper's jaw dropped.

Wow.

Draper was momentarily tongue-tied. For a man who was rarely at a loss for words, that was something.

Finally, he managed to spit out something. "You look beautiful."

"Thank you," Ginny said.

This was the woman who had lived next door to him for three months? The woman of the paint-spattered clothes and the messy bun held in place by a paintbrush?

He felt like he was seeing her for the first time.

She had always been so unapologetically at home on her front porch in her painting duds. And yet she had transformed into such an elegant beauty.

Man, had he been missing out.

Ginny's sense of self-assurance seemed to give

her so much more depth than the women he'd dated, most of whom wouldn't allow him to see them without makeup.

Not only had he made the right decision asking her to accompany him tonight, but he also felt like he'd won the date lottery.

Jerry stuck out his hand for a shake. "Fortune."

"Sanders. Nice to talk to you."

"Take good care of her, okay?"

"You better believe it." Draper offered Ginny his arm and she took it. "Shall we?"

"You kids be home by midnight," Jerry called.

"'Bye, Jerry," Ginny said, with a wave over her shoulder.

The good-natured sparring between them reminded Draper of his relationship with his own siblings. Family was important to him. It was nice to know that she was close to her brother.

"He's funny," Draper said as they made their way down the bricked path. "Good sense of humor."

"He has his moments," she said. "But he really is a good guy."

Draper opened the passenger side door of his Tesla and stayed there until Ginny had settled in. He closed the door, then walked around to the driver's side. After he'd slid behind the wheel, Ginny turned to him and smiled.

"Hi," he said, and regarded her with the same wonder that had hit him when he'd first glimpsed her in the foyer.

"Hi," she answered.

Something passed between them and he had to look away to quell the overwhelming urge to lean in and nuzzle her neck. He craved another whiff of her perfume. When he'd offered her his arm, he'd caught a whisper of something soft and floral with barely there hints of spice. Although, he wasn't completely sure about the spice. After witnessing her transformation from shy girl next door to classic beauty, maybe he was imagining the juxtaposition of sweet and spicy?

He blinked away the thought and his mind raced to come up with something clever to say.

As he started the car and backed out of the driveway, he asked, "Is Jerry your only sibling?"

Not exactly clever, but it would do.

"I have two more brothers," she said. "Scott and Dane."

"Let me guess—" He stole a glance at her and smiled. "You're the baby of the family. Am I right?"

Before she could answer, he looked away, shifted into Drive and they were on their way.

"What makes you think that?" she asked.

"Just a hunch," he answered.

"You're right. I'm the youngest."

"Do your other brothers live in town?"

"They do. They have houses not too far from here."

"And your parents? Are they local?"

"Usually," she said. "But at the moment they're teaching English as a second language in Japan."

"Adventurers, huh?"

She chuckled. "Well, I've never thought of Ellen and Harry Sanders that way, but I suppose it does take an adventurous spirit to pack up and move to the other side of the world. They certainly are having the time of their lives. Neither of them is ready to retire just yet. So it's a good way for them to see the world."

"Sounds ideal."

They were quiet for a moment and Ginny took the opportunity to drink in Draper's profile—the close-cropped light brown curls, the sculpted cheekbones, the perfect patrician nose, his lips—slightly fuller on the bottom than on top. From this angle it gave the appearance of a slight pout, but judging from what she knew of Draper's personality, he wasn't prone to sulking. He seemed too sure of himself for that.

But, jeez, Louise, the sum total of all the parts added up to one great-looking guy. The butterflies swarmed in her abdomen again, causing her to lose her breath for a moment.

Yesterday, she'd been content to scope him out from afar. Now, here she was sitting next to him in his car...his date for the night.

She would allow herself to call it that. Though she wouldn't be at all surprised if she woke up and realized that this was all just a dream. If it was, she would most certainly go back to sleep so she could try to finish it.

Especially since she didn't even know where they were going.

She was about to ask, but he picked that moment to glance over at her and caught her looking at him.

"What?" he said, his eyes crinkling at the corners. Ginny's toes curled in her sandals and she lost her train of thought.

"What about you?" she asked because it was the only thing she could think of, though she was curious. "Do you have siblings other than Beau and Belle? Or is it just the three of you?"

"Oh, heavens, no," he said. "We're a big, boisterous family. I'm one of seven children."

Ginny's eyes widened and Draper nodded. "My folks are Miles and Sarah. They live in New Orleans. In addition to Beau and Belle, there's Nolan, Austin, Georgia and Savannah."

He ticked the names off by tapping the steering wheel with his fingers.

"And that's just my immediate family," he added. "If you factor in all of the Fortune cousins and aunts and uncles, it's mind-boggling."

"The Fortunes are a huge bunch," she said.

"And they seem to be growing every day."

Ginny followed his gaze to the ribbon of road stretched out before them.

"Until a few years ago, my immediate family didn't even realize we were part of that Fortune family. Or at least my siblings and I didn't know. My dad did, but he didn't want to have anything to do with the Fortunes. He had a challenging upbringing separated from the rest of them. It was a point of pride not to be lumped in with the lot of them. But that's a long story and, after yesterday, I'm not going to unload on you again because I'm sure you're not interested in the ugly details."

She shook her head. "I don't mind."

He slanted a glance at her and smiled before returning his attention to the road. "You're really easy to talk to."

Her face warmed and she was glad he was looking at the road now, because she was sure she was blushing.

"Thanks," she said.

There was a lull in the conversation and they rode along in companionable silence for a few moments. Finally, she found the courage, and asked, "Remind me again where we're going tonight? I have to admit I was a little unclear about it."

"It's just this fundraiser," he said. "The Austin Arts Gala."

She'd heard of it. She'd seen advertisements, but it was something so far out of her norm that she'd ignored the details. As an artist herself, or at least someone who was trying to rediscover her inner artist, she felt foolish not knowing more about it and made a mental note to look it up.

She had wondered if she was overdressed, but it

was a gala. And now that she took a second look, Draper was wearing a tux. It occurred to her he always seemed to be dressed in suits when she saw him.

In fact, had she ever seen him dressed in anything else?

It didn't matter because he always looked great.

Tonight, she felt good in this dress with her hair and nails done.

She glanced down at her hands, which had been buffed and moisturized. The paint stains were gone. Her nails were shaped and polished, her once ragged cuticles smooth.

Her hands looked so pretty that for once she didn't have the urge to ball them into fists or sit on them to hide their unkempt appearance.

Her gaze traveled down and landed on her bright red toenails. She was glad she'd gone with a bolder color. The candy-apple-red stood out against the black strappy sandals. She'd almost changed her mind and chosen a French pedi to match her manicure, but Honey had persuaded her by saying red was a sexy color and even if Ginny kept her toes hidden beneath socks and tennis shoes, she would know her toenails were painted red. It would be her own sexy secret.

Honey's method of persuasion had made Ginny blanch at first. Did she really appear so repressed that Honey—sweet Honey, of all people—felt the need to ease her into the shock of sexy red polish on her toes?

She liked the bold color. Maybe she'd make a point of treating herself to monthly mani-pedis. It could be the next step in her New Me plan. Actually, her plan hadn't had a name until now. But why not?

As Honey had said, it was self-care.

What was wrong with feeling good? The way Draper had looked at her when he'd picked her up had been worth every moment of the preparation.

It hit her that this was the first time in ages that she'd wanted a man to look at her, after spending so many years trying to make herself invisible.

She banished the thought.

Her New Me plan wouldn't be solely for Draper's benefit, because after tonight there were no guarantees. She would do this for herself because who knew the simple act of self-care was so healing.

When Draper steered his car into the driveway of the Driskill Hotel, Ginny saw three women wearing ball gowns step out of a limousine.

The sinking realization that the gala was a lot more formal that she'd thought deflated her.

Surrounded by wealthy patrons of the arts, she wanted to kick herself for not asking more questions sooner so she could be better prepared. With each gown-clad woman who disappeared inside the hotel's grand entrance, Ginny felt more and more underdressed.

As they waited for the valet, she imagined herself jumping out of the car and running away…until she remembered that it was all she could do to walk in

Kirby's stilettos. Plus, as soon as the thought went through her mind, one of the valets opened her car door and offered a hand to help her out.

Underdressed or not, there was no turning back now.

But after Draper met her on the other side of the car, his eyes glinted and he smiled at her. "Do you mind if I say again that you look gorgeous?"

Earlier, he'd said she looked beautiful. *Gorgeous* felt like a promotion and she resolved she would wear it like a tiara, drawing on the memory of Draper's appreciative expression to carry her through the night.

Chapter Five

The lobby of the Driskill Hotel was stunning, with its marble floors and stained-glass ceiling that dominated the lobby. Marble columns stood sentry with flowy palm trees in ornate planters. The place was elegant and opulent, and full of old-world charm.

When Ginny had been at the University of Texas, the hotel had been a quick six-minute drive down San Jacinto Boulevard. She and her friends had treated themselves to brunch in the 1886 Café once. It had been fun, but it was also a bit pricy and they hadn't done it again.

A sign in the lobby directed them upstairs to the Driskill ballroom, which was on the mezzanine level. Before they could reach the grand staircase, someone called, "Draper Fortune, is that you?"

An older man and his wife, who was desperately thin and bedecked in a stunning ivory satin gown that looked like a hybrid of a wedding dress and an intricate French pastry, waved to Draper from the area of the lobby just outside of the stained glass.

"That's Mr. and Mrs. English," Draper said. "They're prospective clients. I need to say hello. Do you mind?"

Ginny started to drop her hand from Draper's arm and excuse herself to the ladies room to touch up her lipstick, when he said, "Come with me. I'll introduce you."

Her stomach fluttered. If she'd had any worries that he was embarrassed by her comparatively modest dress, he certainly proved she needn't be concerned.

"Draper, my man, it's wonderful to see you," Mr. English said. "Helen and I are just back from Saint-Tropez."

"Mr. and Mrs. English, how nice to see you," Draper said. "I hope you had a wonderful trip. Please allow me to introduce my date for this evening, Ginny Sanders."

Date for this evening.

That was a loaded introduction. On one hand, he had called her his *date*. Officially making this a *date*. But he had qualified it with "for this evening," which implied it was a onetime engagement. More like a once-in-a-double-blue-moon happening.

He had an extra ticket and he asked me. Just

enjoy yourself and don't spoil it by trying to make it into something it's not.

"Tom English," the man said. "Nice to meet you, Ginny. This is my wife, Helen."

Ginny shook Mr. English's proffered hand and turned to offer a similar greeting to his wife.

Mrs. English, with her platinum-gray bob and Saint-Tropez tan, looked down her tiny nose at Ginny's hand as if Ginny had been part of the waitstaff and was passing a tray of something carb-loaded and completely out of the question.

Giving Ginny's dress a not-so-covert once-over, Helen finally squeezed the tips of Ginny's fingers, then angled her body away from her and toward Draper, effectively cutting Ginny out of the rest of the conversation.

Rude.

Alas, returning the slight would not cancel out Helen English's bad manners. Instead, Ginny lifted her chin and said, "Mr. and Mrs. English, it was lovely to meet you. Draper, if you'll excuse me, I'll be right back."

As she'd originally planned, she found a ladies room in the lobby and touched up her lipstick. By the time she returned, Draper was waiting for her by the grand staircase. Mr. and Mrs. English were nowhere to be seen.

They walked up to the mezzanine level, where the ballroom was located. At the check-in table, a woman was seated there—a pretty brunette wearing an emerald-green gown that matched her eyes. Eyes that appeared to only be for Draper.

"My, don't you look handsome this evening," she said.

"I'll bet you say that to all the guys." Draper smiled his charming smile and played into her flirtation just enough that it wasn't quite inappropriate, but enough not to discourage her.

"I don't know about that," she said. "I'm pretty discerning. I'm Natalie Charles, by the way. How can I help you?"

"I guess we could start with locating my table." Draper handed over the tickets. "Two tickets," Ginny wanted to point out.

One for him. One for me.

But as Natalie handed Draper an information card and program, she was too busy flirting to notice he was there with a date.

Ginny reminded herself how easy it was to get swept up in the undercurrent of Draper Fortune's charm. Whether you wanted to be or not. Wasn't that how she'd felt yesterday? Wow, had it really only been one day since that box of chocolates had landed in her yard and Draper had breezed in, all apologies and appeal?

"You're at table number seven, love," Natalie chirped. "The silent-auction items are along the mezzanine. Please have a look and bid generously. The main event, the art auction, will happen after dinner. Here is your bidding paddle. You can preview the art in the Maximilian Room, just behind you."

"Thank you," he said and turned to Ginny. "Let's go look at the art. I want your input on the best pieces."

"My input?"

"Yes. You're an artist."

"Right, I am an artist, but…"

I paint flower still lifes on my front porch—in thirty minutes or less. But even as the words gathered on the tip of her tongue, she tasted how pathetically unconfident they sounded. Besides, now that she'd been painting the flowers, which she loved, for more than three months, she realized she was into this looser, more Impressionistic technique, than overthinking the watercolor landscapes and portraits she'd done in the past. She may have been out of her element at this gala, but it didn't mean she was any less of a person than Natalie McFlirty, who had rendered her invisible, or the Queen of Saint-Tropez, who had snubbed her. She was just different. Different and painfully out of her element.

"But?" Draper asked.

"I hope you haven't asked me here tonight to advise you on art," she said. "Because if you're looking at art as an investment, then you really should hire a professional to assist you."

"Of course," he said as they stepped into the Maximilian Room. "I'm looking at this as a way to support Austin-area artists, and, perhaps, find something that holds its value. I'm interested in your opinion. You are an artist."

As she watched him walk away, she pushed down the niggling disappointment that he hadn't said her opinion on art wasn't the only reason for the invitation.

The room contained rows and rows of easels lined up like soldiers ready to march in formation.

Where should they start?

She had a few fine art college classes under her belt, but her degree was in education because she'd switched her major in the middle of her freshman year.

However, that first semester she had taken a seminar about the elements of art investment, exploring whether art as business might be a viable career path.

But by the end of her first semester, her world had turned upside down and everything changed, leaving her desperate for something safe and secure.

"Look, I need to be clear that I'm not an expert, but I'm happy to share my opinion."

He smiled that charming Draper Fortune smile and she lost her train of thought.

"Since I haven't yet seen your work," he said, "I'll take my chances."

Refusing to bite on the dangling mention of her work, she asked, "This is all work from local artists, right?"

"I believe so." He opened the program and skimmed a few pages.

"Yes." He pointed to the paragraph detailing the works in the auction. "Tonight we are offering work from the finest artists in the Central Texas art community.' Why aren't you showing your work tonight?"

"As you just said, you've never seen my work," she said. "How do you know it even qualifies?"

"I don't know. I just have a feeling about you."

A feeling? About me?

She rolled her eyes in response. When he laughed, she knew he wasn't being serious.

"Here we go," he said. "The paintings have been produced within the past five years, to give patrons a taste of the artist's style."

"Okay, so we know where the work is from," she said. "Now, we need to establish which genre you're interested in."

"Genre?" He cocked his head to the side and stared at her with those hazel eyes. They were made up of so many colors—blues, greens, browns, ambers—like a kaleidoscope. She stared a little too long before she forced away her gaze and turned toward the first row.

"Do you like portraits, landscapes, still life, scenes of everyday life?" she asked.

He stood beside her and knitted his eyebrows. "I don't know. I guess I'll know what I like when I see it."

She nodded. "Just follow your instincts. The piece of art to buy is one you're in love with."

"I don't fall in love very easily," he said. "But when I do, I fall hard."

His words hung in the air and her stomach flip-flopped.

"How about you, Ginny? Do you fall in love easily?"

Her mouth went dry. Was he talking about art? Something in his tone made her skeptical. She wasn't going to ask because he was, no doubt, teasing her. So instead, she played along.

"I guess I'm a little bit jaded when it comes to falling in love…with art."

She started moving down the aisle, looking at the paintings on the easels. Why had she been so intimidated by him? He really was fun to spar with. She was starting to feel a little powerful.

"Oh, yeah?" he asked. "What happened to you to make you jaded?"

She froze. Well, she had felt powerful, until he'd tossed her kryptonite. She flashed back to the night that changed everything and all the air was sucked out of the room.

Draper had no idea what had happened. It was a long time ago and she wasn't going to let it spoil this night.

"I'll bet you'll fall in love with something tonight," she said. "I've seen some good prospects already."

"I'm pretty picky," he said. "What if I just don't feel it?"

She shrugged. "Then don't buy anything. But that would mean the Austin Art Society would be the big loser of the night."

She purposely held his gaze. He blinked first, as if he was shifting gears back to the reason that they were here.

She moved along and he followed.

"This one is nice." She pointed to an impressionistic landscape of the Texas Hill Country.

"It's nice, but it's a little too pretty for my taste. Tell me what you like about it."

"I know this will sound crazy, but there's something about it that reminds me of the English Moors."

He narrowed his eyes. "But it's Texas."

"Right, but art can be whatever you see. Even though I was born and raised in Texas, I've always loved the romance of the English Moors."

"Have you ever been to England?"

"Only in books."

He did a double take and squinted at her.

Nerd alert! Alas, that was a huge part of who she was and she wasn't going to pretend to be anything else.

"What's your favorite book?" he asked.

"*Wuthering Heights.* Hence my love of the English Moors." She gestured to the painting and they both studied it.

"I've heard of it, but I've never read it," he said. "I know it's a classic."

"Oh, it's wonderful. Equal parts romantic and tragic. I'll lend you a copy."

When he didn't answer, she cringed inwardly.

Nerd overload!

In an attempt to rein in her literary exuberance, she quirked an eyebrow. "I think this piece would complement your current place."

A bark of laughter escaped him. "The Dobson house? Seriously?"

"That's where you're living, isn't it? This painting is done in classic style and has a late-twentieth-century eclectic vibe, like the Dobson interior. No offense to the Dobsons. Their house is thoroughly their taste, which you must like since you haven't changed a thing."

Ugh. That did not come out the way she meant it. She wanted to say it was a classic, comfortable house that matched a classic, accessible painting.

"I'm renting on a short-term basis," he said. "Why would I redecorate?"

"Even for the short term, it's important to make a place yours. Personally, I think the Hill Country landscape is beautiful. But never mind. So show me what you do like."

Draper nodded. When he walked away in search of a good example, she stayed to gaze at the Hill Country painting. A man walked up and stood next to her in front of the little landscape.

He crossed his arms over his chest and tilted his head to the side. "This one's nice."

"It is," she said. "I love the brushwork."

Ginny could feel the man's gaze on her, but she kept her eyes trained on the painting.

"Are you going to bid on it?" he asked.

Before she could answer, Draper appeared at the head of the row of easels. "Ginny, I found one I like."

She watched Draper's gaze travel from her to the man and back to her.

"You can't go wrong with this painting," she said to the guy. "Excuse me, please."

As she made her way to Draper, she couldn't quite sort out his expression.

"So show me this painting," she said. "I'm eager to figure out your style."

The painting was a large abstract of bold, bright colors with accents of black and gold leaf. It was about 180 degrees different from the sweet little landscape she'd pointed out.

After learning that Draper's taste fell along contemporary lines, she helped him select several other paintings to bid on. With that task complete, they looked over the silent-auction offerings, and then made their way to the ballroom.

When they stepped inside, it was as if they had entered a fairy tale wonderland of gold, white and crystal. There were so many flowers, Ginny grappled with the urge to whip out her phone and start taking reference photos to paint. White roses mingled with snowball-size peonies and ranunculus. The white linen-covered tables held more flowers in tall, slender gilded vases, along with white china on gold chargers and gold-toned flatware. The gilded extravaganza was accented by the sleek minimalist look of gold Chiavari chairs.

There were so many flowers, candles in golden mercury glass and tiny twinkling lights that the place looked like something inspired by the Hall of Mirrors at the Palace of Versailles.

She was so far out of her comfort zone that it was at once thrilling and terrifying. She remembered Kirby saying to her once that a comfort zone was a cozy place, but nothing ever grew there.

She must be growing because the entire time she had been at college in Austin, she'd had no idea that this elegant ballroom even existed. It was intriguing to discover it now.

Along the way to their table, Draper stopped to greet another acquaintance. Again, he introduced her as his date for the evening. After initial pleasantries, the conversation turned to business and Ginny took a step back to let them talk. She scanned the ballroom and her gaze was snared by the guy who had appreciated the Hill Country painting alongside her.

He grinned.

She smiled. She hadn't really gotten a good look at him before. Now she could see he was nice-looking in the traditional sense of the word. Not devilishly handsome like Draper, but the guy had blond hair and light eyes. He carried himself as if he was comfortable in a tuxedo.

For that matter, everyone here seemed to be at home in formal wear.

When a server stopped and offered him a flute of champagne, he took two off the tray and brought one to her.

"You look thirsty," he said.

She accepted the glass. "Thank you."

Ha! Thirsty was another slang word the kids in her classes used all too frequently. It had a decidedly derogatory meaning. She was sure he didn't mean it that way. If Draper had said she looked thirsty, it would've surely inspired a round of good-natured banter, but she didn't feel a similar energy with this guy.

She was about to ask him his name when Draper's friend disappeared into the crowd and he turned back to Ginny.

"Sorry about that," Draper said. "Another prospective client."

He stopped short and looked at the guy.

"Hello, I'm Draper Fortune. And you are?"

"Linton Nash."

The men shook hands.

Linton turned to Ginny. "I didn't get your name when we were in the auction-preview room."

"I'm Ginny Sanders." She offered her hand and he held it a couple of beats too long.

"Nice to meet you, Ginny Sanders."

"Well, Linton Nash, it looks like they're starting

to serve dinner," Draper said. "We're going to find our table, if you'll excuse us."

Draper put his hand on the small of Ginny's back as he guided her away from Linton. His touch made her whole body tingle.

"That was the guy who was talking to you when you were looking at the Hill Country landscape." It was more of a statement rather than a question and she wasn't sure what she was supposed to do with it.

"Oh, I guess it was."

"He was hitting on you."

Ginny snorted and was grateful when the sound was swallowed up by the Mozart concerto the orchestra began playing. "Hitting on me? Don't be ridiculous. He happened to like the Hill Country painting and I encouraged him to bid on it. You didn't like that painting. Is there a problem?"

"No problem."

They were the first to arrive at table seven. They found their place cards, and as Draper pulled out the chair for Ginny, he said, "You may think he wasn't hitting on you, but I'll bet you before the night is over he'll make it very clear that's exactly what he was doing."

"No, he won't."

She started to say "He won't, because clearly I'm here with you," but that might imply that she was more than his date for the evening and she didn't want to make things uncomfortable by conflating her seat-filler status with something more serious.

He lowered himself onto his chair. “Yes, he will.”

“Draper.”

“Yes?”

“Would it bother you if he did?”

Something flashed in Draper’s eyes, as if the question had caught him off guard, but then he blinked and the usual mirth that always seem to bubble just beneath the surface returned.

“It won’t bother me if we make a bet and I win,” he said.

“A bet? What kind of a bet?”

“If he hits on you…” Draper held her gaze. She reveled in the license to look at him. “You have to show me your paintings.”

“What?” Ginny said.

“If he hits on you again,” Draper reiterated, “you have to show me your paintings.”

When she didn’t answer, he said, “The ones you create on your porch every day.”

“And if he doesn’t?” Ginny asked.

“I don’t know—what do you want?”

You.

She bit her bottom lip before the word could escape. She did *not* want him. Or at least she shouldn’t want him. She had no earthly idea where that thought had bubbled up from. But even if she could tamp it down, there was nothing she could do about the heat blooming across her face.

She cleared her throat. “I don’t know. This is your brilliant idea. I have no idea what to wager.”

"Okay, if he doesn't hit on you by the time the auction starts, I'll buy you that Hill Country painting."

"No! Absolutely not," Ginny said just as a couple approached their table.

Wonderful. Perfect timing. Scare away your tablemates.

She leaned into Draper. "The opening bid is three hundred dollars, which is way too expensive, and who knows how much it will end up going for."

He smelled expensive. Like cedar and freshly cut grass and citrus. She breathed in, savoring the scent of him, until she realized she might be obvious and sat back into her personal space.

Draper smiled, and she wondered if he knew what she'd been doing. But she didn't care, because the way he was looking at her, once again, had Ginny feeling it all the way down to her red-painted toes.

And then he leaned in and whispered in her ear.

"You look gorgeous tonight. A guy would have to be an idiot not to try."

What kind of a guy would go after another man's date?

Draper was trying not to let Linton Nash ruin his night. But right before dinner he'd glanced over at the table next to theirs and saw the man seated there, apparently dateless. Each time he caught the guy staring at Ginny, Draper warred with the urge to get up and deck him.

Draper reminded himself that he didn't have a claim on her. Until yesterday, they'd only had one very short conversation. And he couldn't even remember what they'd said.

How was it that he had never really seen her until now? The sprinkling of freckles across her nose. The clear sea-glass-blue of her eyes. The sexy pout of her lips that made them seem, oh, so kissable.

Why had he not noticed these things until he had picked her up for their date this evening?

After dinner, as a small ensemble of musicians from the Austin Symphony Orchestra entertained the attendees, the volunteers set up for the live auction. Draper caught Nash watching Ginny again. It was basic good manners to back off once it was clear that the woman was with someone else for the evening, especially when she wasn't actively flirting back. In fact, Ginny seemed oblivious to the guy's glances.

When the ensemble began playing the opening strains of "Moon River," Draper asked Ginny, "Would you like to dance?"

"Thanks, I'd love to," she said.

He took her hand and led her onto the dance floor. Maybe this would make it clear to Nash that she was unavailable for the evening.

They stepped onto the floor and Draper pulled her close. As they swayed to the music, he was surprised by how good Ginny felt in his arms. Most of the women in his orbit were tall model types. Not that he had a type, but it just seemed to work out that way. Ginny was petite, probably a good foot shorter than he was, but she fit…well.

Holding her close, he could smell her shampoo and perfume—that heady floral spicy scent that had first taunted him when they'd gotten into the car earlier this evening. It was intoxicating. She was rather intoxicating. An unexpected awareness shot through him like pins and needles—the best kind of pins and needles. Like acupuncture that released what was ailing him and made him go "Ahhh, that's better."

Granted, comparing someone to acupuncture might not be the most romantic thing to think about… *Wait a second, how did* romantic *even enter into this equation?*

It didn't matter. This was Ginny, his shy, sweet next-door neighbor, who it turned out was not as shy as he'd first thought. She was smart and artistic and had a quick wit…but she was definitely just a friend.

That's what he told himself as he held her and the two of them moved to the music, lost in the moment, until the song ended and he felt a firm tap on his shoulder.

He turned to see none other than Linton Nash standing there. *What the*—fill in the blank with an unsavory word he would never say in front of Ginny—*do you want now?*

Before Draper could edit his words, Linton said, "Hey, buddy, mind if cut in?"

Yeah, buddy, I do. Get lost. But the besotted way

he was looking at Ginny was a cold bucket of reality tossed in Draper's face.

He had no claim on her.

This Linton Nash dude was into her. Who was Draper to stand in the way?

"Sure," he said, swallowing a feeling that begged him to haul off and deck the guy, even though he had no right. Instead, he leaned down and whispered into Ginny's ear, "*Bing, bing, bing.* I believe our wager has a winner. I'll look forward to my private showing of your art."

Ginny glared at him, looking disoriented and less than thrilled to have lost the bet.

Proving that karma was real, the orchestra switched from the slow, romantic melody he and Ginny had danced to into a discordant jazzy rendition of "Happy Together" arranged for xylophone and bass.

Draper found some consolation in the fact that the song was more a musicians' showpiece rather than a dance tune. Even so, it didn't deter Linton Nash from trying. As he and Ginny shuffled around to the up-tempo beat, Draper walked back to their table, trying to ignore the strange feeling in his chest that pulsed between heartbeats.

When the song ended, the gala chair took the stage.

"Let's hear it for the members of the Austin Symphony Orchestra. Weren't they wonderful?" After the applause died down, she said, "The dancing will continue after the auction. For now, if everyone will please take their seats, we're ready to start the auction."

It must've been his lucky night because Draper won the bid on his two favorite abstracts. He really should've been satisfied with that, but when the Texas Hill Country piece came up and Linton Nash placed the first bid, Draper raised his paddle to counter. He had only intended to drive up the price, but with each glare that Nash hurled in his direction, it started to feel personal.

"What in the world are you doing?" Ginny said.

Draper slanted her a glance. "You said you like this painting."

"And you said it wasn't your style," she countered.

"It's not for me." Draper lifted his paddle again. "It's for you."

The auctioneer acknowledged him and upped the bid to $750, then looked at Linton Nash, who shot Ginny a smoldering glance before he lifted his paddle.

Ginny wanted to crawl under the table. Instead, she put her hand on Draper's arm. "Please stop. I can't afford a painting like that. Let Linton have it."

"Not gonna happen." Draper raised his paddle again.

When all was said and done, Draper won the bidding war.

If there was a silver lining, after the auction, Linton Nash left without incident, except for a few glares at Draper. At least he hadn't tried to chat Ginny up or ask for her phone number, putting her in the position of having to decline… She had been girding herself for the possibility.

Now, as Draper steered the car into his driveway, Ginny braced herself for what she hoped wouldn't be an awkward good-night.

The ride home had been mostly silent. Since she'd been in her head for much of the trip home pondering the dance with Draper and his reaction when Linton had cut in. Had the guy truly been interested in her, or had she simply been collateral damage in a clash of titans?

It was hard to say.

Draper had been equally silent. He hadn't mentioned the evening or Nash or the painting, which a porter had stowed in the front trunk space of his car.

Maybe on the way home he'd had time to understand why she couldn't accept such an expensive gift.

She hoped.

He killed the engine, got out of the car and passed the trunk, but didn't retrieve the painting. As he opened her door, she breathed a sigh of relief and realized she was sad for the night to end. She felt like Cinderella at midnight, even though it was getting close to 1:00 a.m.

The painting and Linton Nash's inappropriate advances aside, she'd had a good time tonight. She hoped that despite everything, Draper had enjoyed himself, too.

He offered her his arm and they started toward her house.

His body was warm and solid. The cedar and citrus scent of him tempted her to lean in closer. That in itself was a shift, because it had been a very long time since she'd wanted to be this close to a man, for any reason.

For a split second, she allowed herself to imagine Draper kissing her good-night.

It would start with a gentle embrace and a whisper of fingers over her cheek, and end with a soft brush of lips, an unspoken promise of…of…

No, she was getting ahead of herself.

One step at a time.

At least she felt safe enough to imagine something she hadn't dared dream of since college.

But she wasn't going to think about that right now because they were standing at her front door.

A frisson of anticipation shimmied through her body, and she turned to face him.

"I had a lovely time tonight, Draper. Thank you."

In the dim amber glow of the porch light she watched the corners of his mouth tip up into that dazzling smile that made his eyes crinkle around the edges.

As he tilted his head and leaned toward her, something solid and furry thudded onto the porch. It reared up on its hind legs and planted a sloppy kiss on Ginny's cheek.

It was Otis, the Houdini of black Labs who lived two houses down.

"Otis, down, boy," Draper commanded. When the dog sat, Draper took him by the collar with one hand and scratched under the chin with the other. "What are you doing out at this hour, buddy?"

The spell was officially broken.

"Thanks for going with me." His voice was casual. "I'd better see this wayward child home. 'Night."

As he stood and guided the dog by the collar, he gave a friendly wave.

The starlight had vanished from his eyes. Ginny wondered if it had really been there or if she'd just been caught up in the moment and had imagined it.

Chapter Six

"You were right, Kirbs," Ginny said into the phone. "It was a total Cinderella night. I had such a great time, I haven't quite come down from the high yet."

"I'm so glad you had fun," she said. "When are you going to see him again?"

Ginny's heart clinched as she remembered being kissed by the dog rather than Draper. Even though she had prepared herself for the reality that their date might very well be a one-off, she still hadn't gotten over the fact that if not for Otis, Draper would've kissed her.

And she would've let him.

Instead, Draper had said good night and had taken Otis home.

The dog's intervening was probably for her own good. Kissing a man for the first time in almost ten years was a pretty big deal. In the light of day, she wasn't as sure as she'd been last night that she could have one kiss from Draper Fortune and walk away. Now that she'd had time to process everything, it was clear the way the evening had ended was for the best.

"I don't know," she said. "I don't think I'm his type. If you know what I mean."

"I have no idea what you mean," Kirby said. "You're smart, talented and gorgeous. Basically, you're the whole package. He would be lucky to have you."

Ginny couldn't suppress a smile. "Spoken like a true-blue best friend. Thank you, but have you seen Ines Bartholomew? Long legs, tiny where it matters, ample where it matters more. She is Draper's type."

"Yes, and we saw how that turned out. If the guy is in to playing games then he doesn't deserve you. I don't want you to get hurt, but are you sure it's a one-off?"

As Ginny contemplated whether or not to tell Kirby about the almost kiss and Draper buying the Hill Country painting for 1,750 dollars, saying it was for her but leaving it in the car. Not that she would've accepted it. She took a sip of her coffee. It had gone cold. She had brewed it for breakfast but hadn't finished it. She got up from the kitchen table, opened the freezer and got a few ice cubes. If she could make the best of room-temperature coffee and manage the issues the kids in her classes threw at her, then why couldn't she figure out how to solve the problem of these weird feelings for Draper?

She had really wanted to figure this out on her own, but it seemed to be a lose-lose situation. She couldn't accept it.

Then there was the bidding war/pissing match he'd gotten into with Linton Nash. She couldn't for the life of her figure that out.

The men didn't even know each other. Why were they acting like enemies? Was it just because Linton had asked her to dance?

She had taken care not to encourage the guy since she'd come to the gala as Draper's guest, but when Linton had cut in and asked her to dance—who even did that anymore?—she'd had no choice but to dance with him, because Draper had walked away smug in his glory of proving his point and winning the bet.

"Hello?" Kirby said. "Ginny, are you there?"

"I'm here. Sorry. Okay, so last night was great, but something weird happened."

"Don't tell me he got out of line."

"Of course not. He was a perfect gentleman."

Ginny told Kirby about Linton, the bet that she and Draper had made, and how after Linton had cut in Draper had declared himself the winner.

Kirby laughed. "I wasn't even there and it's pretty clear this Linton dude was hitting on you. So that means that you get to see Draper when he comes over to see your paintings. Maybe it was just a ruse to see you again…though I don't understand why he couldn't just ask you out."

"Wait, there's more."

She told Kirby about the Hill Country painting.

"He said he bought it for me because I liked it."

"Stop it. The guy bought you a seventeen-hundred-dollar painting?"

"No. I refused to accept it. I'm not going to take an expensive gift when, basically, it wasn't even really a date. He needed an escort for the evening and I happened to be in the right place at the right time."

Kirby snorted. "You'd better be careful how you're throwing around the words *escort* and *expensive gifts*."

"Eww," Ginny said. "No. Just no."

"I'm sorry." Kirby chuckled. "I couldn't resist."

Ginny made a sound that wasn't quite a laugh, but it wasn't a groan, either. "I know he didn't mean it the way it seemed, but at the end of the night, I didn't have to refuse it because he left it in the car. That's a good thing because I didn't want to give Draper the wrong idea. I'm just not ready to go there after what happened with Trey."

His name seemed to echo in the ensuing silence, tainting the way she'd longed for Draper to kiss her last night.

"You don't owe any man anything. Even if you had accepted the painting—and I'm not saying you should've—you wouldn't have owed him anything else. You didn't ask him to buy it for you."

"No, I didn't. Really, I think this was more about getting the best of Linton Nash than buying me for the night. And there's another side to it. I think Draper might just be a generous guy. He bought three paintings at the auction without flinching. I told you how he bought Ines that bracelet. I don't know that he realizes how expensive gifts can be misconstrued."

Someone rang the doorbell.

"Hey, Kirbs, I need to go. But I'll drop off your dress at the dry cleaner tomorrow on my way to school. Thanks again for being my fairy godmother. I love you."

"Love you, too. Talk soon."

Ginny dropped her phone into the pocket of her pink seersucker robe and padded down the hall. When she opened the door, Draper was standing there holding the Hill Country painting.

He grinned. "Hi."

"Hi." She smiled and pulled the robe closed. It was only nine o'clock on Sunday morning, but she wanted to kick herself for not getting dressed sooner. To cover her embarrassment, she resorted to sarcasm. "May I help you?"

"I hope so," he said. "You forgot something last night."

He held out the painting. Its ornate gilded frame was visible through the bubble wrap.

"Oh, no, I didn't forget it. That belongs to you."

"Nope. I don't like this painting. You do."

"Then you shouldn't have bid on it. You bought

it, you…" She was trying to think of a play on the phrase "you broke it, you bought it," but she came up blank. "You bought it, you—you keep it. But thank you for a nice evening last night. I need to go before my coffee gets warm."

"Cold," he said.

She frowned at him. Was he calling her cold? *The nerve.*

"You said you have to go before your coffee gets warm. Don't you mean before it gets cold?"

She scrunched up her face. "No. I'm drinking iced coffee."

"Oh. Well, that sounds good. Can I have one?"

She shook her head and a laugh broke through her scowl.

"You are something else, aren't you?" she said. "I can see why you're successful in snagging clients. Come in. But I'm not accepting the painting."

She started down the hall toward the kitchen and he followed.

"I was thinking we could make a trade," he said.

"I'm not trading you a cup of coffee for your painting," she said as she filled the coffeepot with water.

"We'll see," he said.

She was measuring coffee into the filter and stopped mid-scoop.

"'We'll see'?" she repeated. "What? Are you going to sneak it into my house in the middle of the night and leave it?"

He shrugged. “That’s a thought.”

She felt her cheeks flame at the thought of Draper in her house—in her bedroom—in the middle of the night.

She pushed the brew button and pushed the thought out of her head. The pink blanket that had been draped over the arm of his sofa popped into her mind. She remembered how he’d said he and Beau had made a game out of pawning it off on each other, leaving it in unexpected places in each other’s houses. Her stomach tightened at the thought of Draper and her being so familiar with each other that they would carry on like that.

But somehow, playing “hide the art” with an expensive painting didn’t seem viable.

“Did Otis get home okay last night?”

“Eventually. I didn’t want to ring the Billings’ doorbell in the middle of the night so Otis spent the night in my garage and I took him home this morning.”

“It was good of you to keep him safe.”

He shrugged like it was nothing. “So what exactly do you paint?” He glanced around the kitchen. “And do you have any of your work hanging in the house?”

“I paint flower still lifes.” The admission made her shrink a bit, because what was the chance that Draper, the abstract lover, would connect with what she painted. The thought of him seeing her work made her feel shy.

“Why don’t you have any of your work hanging

in your own home?" he asked. "I'd think that would be your most important gallery."

She shrugged. "I guess I've never thought of it that way. And really, I'm just getting back into painting. I haven't done it in years."

"Why not?"

She imagined what he would do if she unloaded the real reason—if she told him that something very ugly had tainted what she'd once loved the most in the world.

"It's a long story. It's personal and I don't want to talk about it. Okay?"

"Oh. I'm sorry. Of course."

Way to go, Ginny. Way to shut things down and make it awkward.

The coffeemaker hissed and spit as it drained the hot liquid into the carafe. When it was done a moment later, Ginny poured it into a mug. "For the best iced coffee, it has to come to room temperature. Normally, I have some cold brew in the fridge, but I haven't had a chance to make a batch this morning. It'll take a while for this to cool. Or would you just like it hot?"

"I can wait," he said. "Unless I'm keeping you from something."

"No. You're not." She blurted the words before she could think better of it.

She was a bundle of conflicting emotions. On one hand, she had papers to grade and lesson plans to update. Not to mention today's painting to do. But

Draper Fortune, with his easy smile and quick wit, made her want to while away this Sunday morning, drinking coffee and talking about everything and nothing.

She wasn't even dressed, while he was sitting at the kitchen table in his crisp white oxford shirt and khakis, looking so comfortable in his own skin.

Looking so breathtakingly sexy that sometimes she lost her words or blurted out the exact opposite of what she meant…or, even worse, exactly what she did mean.

"Then I'll wait. Tell me about your process."

"My process? I set up an easel and I paint flowers."

That was inspired.

"Yes, but what inspires you?"

"What?" He had this uncanny way of almost reading her mind.

"The question is self-explanatory. Where do you get your inspiration?"

"It's not really that exciting or revolutionary," she said. "I love flowers, so I paint them."

She stopped. He was trying to make conversation and she was nervous and making this harder than it had to be.

"I like to try and capture their beauty," she said. "I've found the best way for me to do that is to paint fresh flowers rather than pictures of flowers in quick studies, so that I don't overthink or over complicate things. Although, I so wanted to snap some photos of the flowers last night. Those white peonies were gorgeous."

He nodded. He was watching her in a way that made her wish she could read his thoughts, like he so effortlessly seemed to do with hers.

"So that trade I was talking about," he said. "What if you traded one of your paintings for the Hill Country piece?"

"You haven't even seen my work, Draper. How do you know it's something you'd want to trade a seventeen-hundred-dollar painting for?"

"Then let me see it." He smiled sheepishly. "Actually, if I'm being completely honest, the reason I came over this morning was to collect on my bet."

He smiled as if he had just played the winning card.

She shook her head. "I don't think—"

"You can't go back on your word. I won the bet fair and square, when Nash asked you to dance. He hit on you and I intend to collect on the wager."

She fidgeted with the sash on her robe. "I have no intention of going back on my word."

But she'd also hoped he'd just been humoring her and hadn't been serious about following through. "I want to set up a proper showing for you. I'll need a couple of days to get everything in order."

"A couple of days?" he asked. "Then Tuesday it is."

On Monday afternoon, as Draper stopped by the office to pick up a prospectus for a client in Houston, the peonies in the window of Petunia's Posies stopped him.

They reminded him of Ginny and how she'd said she wanted to photograph the peonies at the gala so she could paint them.

He paused and studied the flowers' delicate beauty.

They were breathtaking.

No wonder Ginny drew inspiration from fresh floral arrangements. He lingered, trying to see the flowers through her eyes, trying to imagine how she would paint them.

The display in the window included a chalkboard with artfully drawn fun facts about the peony. When he read that they symbolized bashfulness, he knew he had to go in and get a bunch for Ginny to paint, even though the more he got to know her, the less shy she seemed.

Other common peony meanings included prosperity, good fortune, riches, honor and compassion.

Oh, and romance and a happy marriage, too, but so many meanings were assigned to the blossom, it seemed like a choose-your-own significance.

He chose shyness.

He opened the shop's door and stepped inside. Floral-scented air greeted him. It had been a long time since he'd been inside a florist's. Usually, he had flowers sent, but the ones he'd sent in the past were for an entirely different reason than this impulse.

Did peonies also represent purity?

It didn't matter.

Ginny loved to paint fresh flowers. If he gave her something to paint, maybe she would feel more comfortable sharing her work with him.

Getting a look at her art had become a challenge.

And there were few things Draper loved more than overcoming a challenge.

"Hello, Mr. Fortune," said a woman who popped out from behind an open cooler door. The glass was fogged, so he hadn't noticed her right away. But there she stood, arms full of the long-stemmed roses she was adding to a green bucket in the cooler.

She'd called him by name.

New Orleans was such a large, bustling city, that Draper had enjoyed relative anonymity outside of his social circles. In Rambling Rose, he hadn't gotten used to people he'd never met knowing his name. Every time he ventured into a local business, at least one person greeted him by name. That made it all the more important to treat each person with kindness and enthusiasm. Because at one point, the Fortunes had not been so welcome in this town.

"Hello there," he said and flashed his best smile. "Your magnificent window display stopped me in my tracks. I had to come in and buy a bouquet of those gorgeous peonies."

The woman's eyes flashed and sparkled. "Of course. I'm happy to help you." She gently placed the roses inside the cooler and shut the door.

Wiping her hands on her green apron, she said,

"My name is Margaret, by the way. Petunia—she's the owner, obviously," she grinned, "did that display. So, let's talk about this bouquet—are these flowers for someone special?"

"They're for a friend."

He started to explain that they were for Ginny to paint, but the look on Margaret's face stopped him.

"A friend. I see. Would you like them delivered? If your friend lives in town, I can get them there before noon. You could even add a note if you'd like."

Looking hopeful, Margaret raised her eyebrows and pointed to a rack of small cards on the counter next to a teddy bear holding a heart that said "I love you."

Draper knew what Margaret was doing. She was about as subtle as a skywriting airplane. The last thing he needed to do to Ginny was give the locals reason to think there was more going on here than what was really happening. That they were…a thing.

Something tightened and dipped in his stomach at the thought. He chalked up the odd sensation to concern for his neighbor. She didn't seem romantically interested in him and he didn't want to create a messy rumor that she would have to clean up.

"No, thank you, Margaret. If you wouldn't mind wrapping them up, I'll take them with me and deliver them myself. In fact, if you don't mind, I need to run down to my office for something. I'll be back in five minutes to pick them up."

Twenty minutes later, Draper was standing on Ginny's front porch knocking on the door.

When she answered and saw the flowers, her eyes flew open wide.

"I come bearing gifts of inspiration for today's painting session," he said. "You haven't already painted, have you?"

He handed her the large bouquet of pink and white peonies, which Margaret had wrapped in white tissue paper and tied with matching pink and white ribbon.

Cradling the bouquet in her arms, she bent her head down and closed her eyes as she inhaled.

The angle of her face gave him a clear view of that sweet spray of freckles that danced across her nose. He smiled at the sight of her in her cotton dress and sandals.

Ginny was a breath of fresh air. Especially compared to other women who had come and gone from his life. She had turned down an expensive painting, but seemed over the moon over a large bunch of flowers.

She looked up and smiled at him. "I got home from school later than usual. I haven't had a chance to paint. I haven't even had a chance to change clothes. But, oh, Draper, peonies are my favorite flower. How did you know?"

"Hey, am I good or what?"

"You're good. Yes, you are. Will you come in? I was just pouring some iced tea."

She held open the door, and as he entered, a

strange feeling, similar to the one he'd experienced in the flower shop, gripped him again. Only this time, the sensation hit him higher in his chest and kicked against his ribs, making his heart thud.

As they walked, his gaze dropped to her feet and he glimpsed the fiery red polish on her toes and remembered how sexy she'd looked at the gala the other night, and how she'd felt in his arms as they'd danced. Had it only been two nights ago?

"I'm going to put these in some water," she said as she took a crystal vase down from a cabinet. "Would you mind grabbing another glass? You can get ice from the dispenser in the fridge and the tea is in the pitcher on the table. It's sweet tea. I hope you don't mind. It's my weakness." She nodded to the cutting board next to the pitcher. "There's some fresh mint from my garden and lemon slices, too."

"This is pretty fancy for afternoon tea." As he dispensed ice into his glass, he watched her carefully arrange the peonies in the vase, which she'd half filled with water.

"That's just how I roll." She punctuated the statement with a smile and a shrug.

That. That right there was what he loved about her.

Er…liked about her.

That unpretentious sweetness. She saw the beauty in fresh flowers, homemade sweet tea with lemon and mint grown in her own garden.

"Would you like to take the tea out onto the front porch?" she suggested. "We can sit on the swing."

"That sounds like fun," he said as he mentally added "appreciates front porch swings" to his list of Ginny's cute attributes. He tried to remember if he had ever sat on a front porch swing, and as far as he knew, he hadn't. The rambling New Orleans Garden District house he'd grown up in had the traditional side porches that were a hallmark of New Orleans architecture, but his family had never spent much time out there and they certainly didn't have a swing.

It was a beautiful afternoon, with a cloudless blue sky and the kind of gentle breeze that made a person long to linger outdoors.

The seat of the swing was covered with a floral-print cushion. A row of smaller coordinating cushions lined the back and sides, taking up space so that their arms touched after they sat down.

They soon found their rhythm, a coordinated pushing-off with their toes and a subtle lifting of feet at just the right pace to keep the motion going. After a short while, it became second nature.

"This is nice," Draper said.

"It is," Ginny said. "I love to read out here."

"Wuthering Heights?" he asked, thinking of how she had said the Hill Country reminded her of the moors in her favorite book.

"Among other books," she said.

"Would you lend me a copy of *Wuthering Heights*?" he asked. "I've never read any of the Brontë sisters."

"Well, extra points to you for knowing a Brontë wrote it."

"Spoken like a true teacher," he said.

She smiled. "I'd be happy to lend you a copy. Mine is at school. I'll bring it home for you tomorrow."

"Sounds like a plan."

She smiled up at him shyly and then looked away. For a moment, they sat in companionable silence. It was nice just being with someone rather than having to fill every moment with empty talk.

Even so, he was the first to speak. "So you went to the University of Texas. And you majored in education with an emphasis on literature."

She nodded.

"Why teaching and not fine art?"

He felt her stiffen—or maybe he sensed it—and then she seemed to disappear inside herself for a moment.

"Oh, well, you know how it goes," she finally said. "I needed to do something practical so that I could support myself. Both of my parents are educators and I love kids. So teaching seemed like a no-brainer."

The words made sense, but they sounded a little canned. He got the feeling that she was leaving something out. He might not have noticed if she hadn't closed the door yesterday and made it clear that she didn't want to talk about why she'd quit painting until this year.

"I saw your work at Kirby's Perks," he said.

"Ginny, you're talented. I had a feeling you were, but now I know you are. I'm not sure what happened that made you quit painting, but I hope you won't deny the world of your talent any longer."

Her eyes went wide. She looked like she wanted to say something, like she was warring with herself. Then, he saw her shut down as clearly as if someone had drawn a blind over her face. He wanted to reach out and pull her close. He wanted to hold her and kiss that spray of freckles on her nose. Hell, he wanted to do a lot more than that.

Instead, Draper stood. "I'd better let you get to work on today's painting. Thanks for the tea."

He took a long pull, finishing the last of his drink and trying to quench his strange sudden thirst for this woman.

Today was the day of Ginny's first private art show.

A string of nerves bunched and knotted in her stomach as she set down her school tote bag on the bench in the mudroom of her house. She paused to pull out the copy of *Wuthering Heights* to give to Draper and put it on the kitchen table after she entered the room.

She glanced at her phone. It was 3:45 p.m. After Draper had left yesterday, she realized they hadn't established a specific time for him to come over and see her work.

Yesterday, when he'd come to the door with the peonies—even at the thought, her stomach slipped out of its knot, performed a little cha-cha, and re-tangled itself—he hadn't mentioned the bet.

But since he'd seen her work in Kirby's, she wondered if maybe he'd realized her paintings were too Texas Hill Country for his taste. Maybe the peonies were a consolation prize of sorts. A way of saying "thanks, but I'll pass on the private show."

She had almost talked herself into trading her artwork for the painting. Sunday, after he'd suggested the trade, a memory of one of her most influential teachers had bubbled up. *Value your work. If you don't value it, why should anyone else?*

For a solid twenty-four hours, she'd cloaked herself in those words, holding them close, convincing herself that it would be pretty cool for her work to be in Draper's collection, because even if nothing came of this energy that seemed to vibrate between them, at least he would think of her every time he looked at her painting.

But yesterday, the way he'd virtually bolted after he'd confessed he'd gotten a preview of her work... well, she hadn't known what to make of things.

He'd shown up at her door with flowers. Beautiful peonies. Her favorite flower.

They'd taken their tea onto the porch and sat on the swing talking while they drank it.

It had seemed so sweet, as if he was trying to court her.

Maybe that misconception was her first mistake.

Did guys even court women anymore? Especially

guys like Draper? She couldn't imagine a woman like Ines being courted.

On one hand, it seemed as if he had made a point of seeing her every day since the gala—actually, it had been every day since Friday.

Today, if he showed, would make five days in a row.

And she kept coming back to those beautiful flowers. They seemed more than a neighborly gesture.

On the other hand, his visits had been short. It wasn't as if he had asked her to dinner. Why did he keep coming around?

Draper didn't seem like the type who would just not show without informing her that he'd changed his mind. But did she know him as well as she thought she did?

Today would tell.

In the meantime, she would set up the exhibit of her work exactly as she'd planned.

She went out to her car and unloaded the easels she'd borrowed from the school's art club. It didn't take long to set them up along the front porch—five canvases displayed on each easel.

When everything was set up, she took a step back and surveyed the exhibit. As she viewed all of the paintings together, a sensation that felt an awful lot like pride bloomed in her chest.

Not too shabby.

Ninety-four paintings in all. Viewed separately, they might look like some sort of painter's shorthand—a warm-up hinting at the mere suggestion of a flower arrangement—but together, they made sense.

Strength in numbers.

If Draper still wanted to trade, he would need to take more than one painting.

Maybe three or five?

They'd cross that bridge if and when they came to it.

She stole a glance at Draper's empty driveway, then physically turned away, casting out the worry that he'd gotten tied up with a client, or maybe he'd even forgotten.

No. It was early yet.

She walked the length of the porch again and debated whether to cover the easels with drapes to make the big reveal more dramatic.

Was that cheesy…or did it show she valued her work?

As she silently debated with herself, she stole another glance over at Draper's house.

To quiet the voice in her head that kept saying "he's not going to show," she covered the easels and decided that, rather than standing here making herself sick with worry, she would go inside, touch up her makeup, change out of her khaki pants and knit shirt and into the new dress she'd bought for the occasion.

On her lunch break, she'd gone over to a boutique in downtown Rambling Rose in search of a new dress. As luck would have it, the sleeveless pink-and-rose medallion-print maxi was the first dress she'd tried on and she'd loved it. It was boho sexy in its free-spirited simplicity, but understated enough that it didn't look like she was trying too hard.

She paired it with the bangle bracelets she loved but hadn't worn in years and a pair of gold hoop earrings her parents had given her for Christmas one year.

As if fate was on her side, just as she was coming downstairs in her new dress, a knock sounded on the door. Her heart leaped and cheered.

Draper was standing on the porch with a bottle of wine.

She was so relieved, it was all she could do to keep from throwing her arms around his neck and kissing him.

"Hi," she said.

"Hi, yourself," he said. He gave her an appreciative once-over. "You look fabulous. Here, I brought this for you…for us. I figured an art show deserved some good wine. I hope you drink red."

I would drink muddy-water if you offered it.

"Yes. Thank you. Come in and I'll get us some glasses."

He hesitated and shot a glance at the covered easels. "I can't wait for the big unveiling."

For a split second, nerves threatened to eclipse the confidence that had bolstered her earlier.

Art was subjective.

Her style might not be for him. Then again, maybe

it was. At least his enthusiasm encouraged her to step out of her comfort zone. Two weeks ago, the thought of showing her work like this would've sent her hiding under her bed.

This was a huge step and she was so grateful to him for it.

They opened the wine and brought the bottle and glasses out to the porch.

Draper poured them each a glass and then toasted Ginny.

"To you. May this be the beginning of many good things for you and your art."

"You haven't even seen my work yet," she said.

He laughed. "Yes, I did, remember? At Kirby's Perks. How much longer are you going to keep me waiting?"

These floral still lifes were different from the watercolor portraits and landscapes hanging up in Kirby's. The watercolors were more realistic—as realistic as watercolor could be. The flowers were more abstract. While she liked both styles, the watercolors took her back to that first semester in college…a time in her life she'd rather forget.

The freedom of expression she felt when she painted the looser floral abstracts transported her forward and didn't allow her the time to move back.

Still, showing her work to Draper seemed so… personal.

Her heart thudded as she removed the covers.

"These are... *Wow!*" he said as he bent forward for a closer look. "Do you mind if I—"

He gestured to the painting and Ginny nodded.

He set down his wine and carefully picked up one of the paintings by its edges. As he squinted his eyes and studied it, Ginny pulled the drapes from the other easels.

Draper returned the painting to its place and then slowly and silently walked the length of the porch, taking his time to look at her work.

Ginny wished she could bottle the way she felt right now—it was like bubbles in a magnum of champagne that had been shaken and was waiting for someone to pop the cork. She struggled to contain her joy.

Finally, Draper said, "Wow. I am blown away. I mean, I knew you were good after what I saw at Kirby's. But—"

Ginny smiled. "Did you know that Kirby is my best friend?"

"I didn't when I went into the coffeehouse, but I did by the time I left. But even before we put two and two together—that I'm the guy you went out with on Saturday and that she's your buddy—I commented on the watercolors she had hanging up in the shop. You know, you really should hire her to do PR for you because she did a great job selling your work. But I guess that wasn't hard because it really is good, Ginny. You're so talented."

So many thoughts were racing through her head

that she didn't even know what to say. Why didn't Kirby tell her that she'd talked to Draper?

Obviously, Draper Fortune had his own tastes and opinions. His tastes did not include the Hill Country painting, which rubbed closer to Ginny's more impressionistic style than it did to his modern abstracts, but he was so enthusiastic about what he was seeing now.

"There are a couple of things I want to tell you about," he said, pulling her from the mire of her musings. "Today, one of my clients mentioned a new gallery in Austin, and I immediately thought of you. You should make an appointment to show them your work."

Ginny blinked at him, still trying to sort out her thoughts. She was at once ecstatic and petrified by the thought of showing her work to a gallery owner. If showing her work to a man who had become… What had Draper become to her? What were they? All the signs seemed to point that maybe, just maybe, they were beginning to think of each other as—dare she say—something more than friends.

Enough about that.

If showing her work to Draper had been this excruciating, what would it be like to show it to a stranger? But…would Draper suggest it if he didn't believe in her?

Stop overthinking it.

"Also, I want you to meet my friend Mackenzie Cole when she's in town next week. Macks is a family friend. She owns a couple of art galleries in New Orleans. She's going to be in Austin a week from Saturday. One of the museums is honoring her for her support of women in the arts. I'll find out more and get us tickets."

Ginny was still speechless, but somehow she managed to reply. "That sounds fabulous. I can't wait to meet her. Draper, do you really think she'll like my work?"

"If I thought there was the slightest chance that she wouldn't love your style, I wouldn't set you up for rejection. I mean, what's not to love?"

Before she could think better of it, Ginny threw her arms around Draper and hugged him. In the process, she accidentally sloshed some wine onto his suit jacket.

She pulled back and swiped at the spot, inwardly thanking the heavens that the red wine only appeared as a wet blotch on the lapel of his dark suit. "Oh, no. I'm so sorry. Let me go inside and get a cloth to—"

When she looked up at him, she realized his arms were still around her waist and the way he was gazing down at her, he didn't look angry about the spill at all. In fact, he looked like she might get that kiss from Draper after all…

He lowered his head and his lips were a hair away from hers when the sound of the front door opening and banging shut had her jerking out of Draper's arms.

"Hey, Ginny, did you have any thoughts on dinner?" It was Jerry. "Oh, hey. Sorry. I didn't mean to interrupt."

Jerry turned on her heel and went back inside, but the moment was gone. Again.

Chapter Seven

The next morning, as Draper parallel-parked his Tesla in front of the downtown Fortune Investments office, his phone rang. Since he didn't recognize the number, he let the call sail over to voice mail.

After he killed the engine, he heard the notification of a voice mail on his phone. He picked up the message, with the hope that it was a potential client in Houston finally returning his call.

"Hi, Draper, this is Natalie Charles. We met the other night at the Austin Arts Gala. I was the one who checked you in. Or, dare I say, I checked you out while I was checking you in. Sorry, I couldn't resist. I don't usually do this, but I got your number from the gala registration. I was wondering if you'd like to get together for a drink sometime. I'm looking forward to hearing from you. 'Bye."

Well, that was...proactive.

And a little bit gutsy. He had to admire her spirit, but he was slammed this week. There was no time for a drink, and frankly, he just wasn't feeling it.

He vaguely remembered her, but he couldn't really recall her in detail.

Nonetheless, he owed it to her to call and decline her invitation. Didn't he?

He'd do that later.

As he got out of the car, he slid the phone into his pocket, and walked around to the passenger side to get the paintings that Ginny had traded him yesterday for the Hill Country piece. He was going to Austin later today and wanted to have them framed so he could hang them up.

He held them gingerly as he let himself inside the office.

"Good morning," his brother Beau said.

"It is a good morning," Draper answered.

"What are you so happy about?" Beau asked.

"Let me show you," Draper said. "I saw Ginny Sanders's work yesterday. She is an incredibly talented artist. I feel like I've discovered a superstar."

Beau got up and walked over to Draper's desk, where he was laying out the paintings side by side.

"Nice." He took a moment to regard each one and nodded his approval before he returned to his desk.

"All this time, she was living next door and we didn't know," Draper said. "I mean, who knew?"

Draper told Beau about the events that had transpired over the last five days, since Ines had tossed the chocolates into Ginny's yard. He waited for his brother to answer, but he was absorbed by something on his computer screen.

"You and Sofia really should come over and have a look at her work. You might even want to commission a painting for your new place. I think she's going to be a big name as soon as she starts showing in the right places."

When Beau didn't respond, Draper glanced down at Ginny's paintings. The sight of them brought him back to her front porch.

Yesterday, he had snapped into business mode after Jerry had interrupted their near kiss. Even though Draper had been burning with the desire to kiss her, now that his head was clear he knew it was a good thing that Jerry's arrival had preempted it.

The desire had been real—and still was, if the tightening in his gut was a sign—ever since he had held her in his arms when they'd danced on Saturday night. He couldn't stop thinking about how perfectly she'd fit and how good she'd felt. He couldn't stop wondering if that bee-stung bottom lip of hers tasted like honey.

But Ginny wasn't like the other women he'd dated. He sensed she was someone who was into long-term relationships and happily-ever-after, like in the books she loved so much. Even though he was attracted to her, he wasn't sure he could give her what she needed. Right now, they were friends. He enjoyed spending time with her and he didn't want to ruin it. When was the last time he'd sat on a front porch swing and shared sweet tea with a woman?

Never.

He'd always been attracted to model types and women-of-the-world, who expected never-ending Dom Pérignon Rosé Gold on charter flights to Paris.

Ginny was like a breath of fresh air. She was refined but not worldly. She had her feet planted firmly on the ground...and she knew how to brew homemade sweet tea that tasted like nectar of the gods.

For those reasons, it was fine if they took things slowly. In fact, it was more exciting than sleeping with a beauty queen on the first date.

If he had learned nothing else, it was that Ginny Sanders was worth the wait.

After Jerry had gone inside yesterday, Ginny was the one who had brought up the idea of trading some of her paintings for the Hill Country painting. Because hers were small, she had wanted him to choose five of her florals.

Even though he would've loved to own any of the nearly one hundred paintings on display, Draper had narrowed it down to three and warned her not to undervalue her work. Their trade set the price of Ginny's paintings at nearly 600 dollars each, if you compared it to the 1,750-dollar price tag of the auction painting.

Ginny seemed happy with the Hill Country painting, and he felt like he'd gotten a good deal.

"So I'm going to introduce Ginny to Macks when she's in Austin. Are you and Sofia going to the museum event? If so, maybe you two and Ginny and I can go together."

Beau smiled at the mention of Sofia's name. He didn't just smile, he seemed to glow from the inside out.

"Yes, I'd love for Macks to meet Sofia, since she will be invited to the wedding," Beau said.

Draper nodded. "You know, it's great to see you so happy."

"Well, there's nothing like the love of a good woman to fix what's ailing you," Beau said.

Draper shrugged. While he could appreciate the change in his brother, he'd really never experienced it for himself.

"I used to equate settling down with the old ball and chain," Beau said. "It seemed like tying myself to one person for the rest of my life was a blueprint for unhappiness, for disaster. I could look at Mom and Dad and see that it was possible, but it always seemed just out of my grasp. That's because before Sofia, I hadn't met the right person."

Beau was right. Their parents, Miles and Sarah, were the perfect example of what was right about marriage. Even after several decades, they seemed to fall deeper and deeper in love with each passing day. But Beau was also right in that their parents' love seemed rare. It wasn't the kind that came along every day. Their oldest brother, Austin, learned that lesson the hard way. Even though he hadn't given up on love and had eventually met his wife, Felicity, the train wreck that was his first marriage had left an indelible impression on Draper. In fact, because of Austin's horrific experience—and the way it had bled over to affect their entire family—Draper had decided marriage wasn't for him.

"When are you going to settle down?" Beau's question landed like a sucker punch.

Draper smiled to hide the niggling discomfort of his brother practically reading his mind. "Me?"

Beau made an exaggerated show of looking around their small office. "Yeah, you. I don't see anyone else in the room."

Draper held up his hands and shook his head, as if warding off a curse. "Yeah, no. I'm happy for you and Sofia, but marriage isn't in the cards for me."

For some outrageous reason beyond his comprehension, an image of Ginny flashed before his eyes. He wasn't sure if it was in a good way, either. Sweet tea and front porch swings in the tiny town of Rambling Rose…it was an interesting contrast to the life he was used to, but he couldn't quite be sure he could take a lifetime of it. Even if Ginny's lips tempted him like the sweetest honey.

Suddenly, he couldn't breathe.

"You might want to try thinking outside your usual box," Beau said. "You're going to be thirty-five pretty soon. That means you'll be on the downward slide toward the big four-oh. The older you get, the faster it goes. You don't want to end up alone."

"Whoa, wait. What?" Draper gave his head a sharp shake. "You don't have to make me sound so pathetic."

"Well…?" Beau gave him a look that seemed to suggest "if the shoe fits."

Draper shrugged. "You can't force these things."

"Right, but you'll never meet anyone if you close your mind to the idea," Beau said.

"So far, I haven't met anyone who is wife material. Women like Sofia are a rare find. You're lucky."

"Yes, I am. I'm very fortunate to have met her, but that's not what we're talking about. So don't try to change the subject. Your problem is you date the wrong women. You need to open your mind and look beyond the glitz and glam. You need someone like… Ginny. A woman like that is wife material. A woman like Ines is not. I mean, who knows, she might make someone a great wife, but if you're looking for what Sofia and I have, you're not going to find that with the party girls you usually date."

No. No, no, no. Draper hadn't heard the rest of what his brother said. His mind had stopped at Ginny.

"I—I can't date Ginny," Draper stammered.

"Why not?" Beau asked. "You light up when you talk about her. If you could've seen yourself just a few minutes ago when you were gushing about her art—"

Draper crossed his arms. "I wasn't gushing. I don't gush."

"You were gushing, bro. I have it from reliable sources that the two of you looked pretty cozy on her front porch swing the other day."

"Who told you that?"

"It doesn't matter who said what," said Beau. "She's a great woman. I don't understand why you're balking."

"I'm balking because Ginny and I are just friends."

Even though I wanted to kiss her.

Oh, dear God. He had almost kissed her. What was wrong with him?

"Since when have you been friends with a woman?"

Draper sighed, then backpedaled. "Okay, the gala was definitely not a date. Ines got mad at me. I had the extra ticket and I didn't want it to go to waste. Come on, it was a business event and I made some good contacts that night. I ran into Tom and Helen English. You know how long I've been working to get their business. I have a meeting with them next Thursday."

"If it was only about business, why didn't you go alone?" Beau leaned back in his chair and laced his hands behind his head, as if he had just drilled the winning serve.

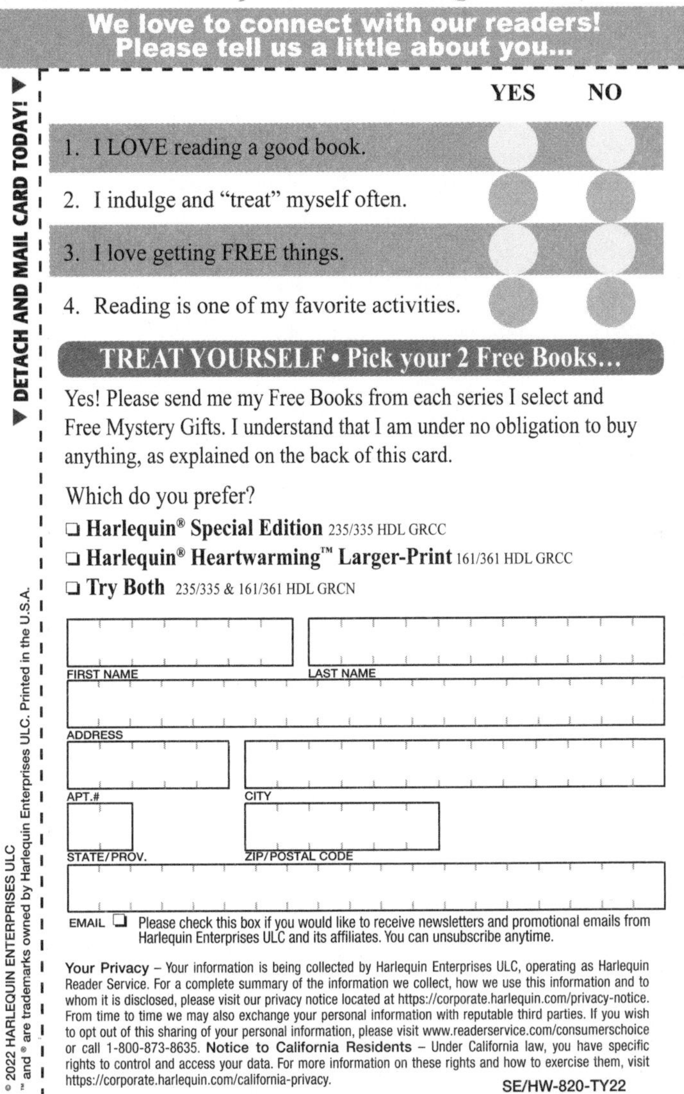

If offer card is missing write to: Harlequin Reader Service, P.O. Box 1341, Buffalo, NY 14240-8531 or visit www.ReaderService.com
BUSINESS REPLY MAIL
FIRST-CLASS MAIL PERMIT NO. 717 BUFFALO, NY
POSTAGE WILL BE PAID BY ADDRESSEE
HARLEQUIN READER SERVICE
PO BOX 1341
BUFFALO NY 14240-8571
NO POSTAGE NECESSARY IF MAILED IN THE UNITED STATES

"You know what those events are like," Draper said. "It's more fun to go with someone. In fact, they can be kind of excruciating if you're solo."

Though Linton Nash seemed to think the gala was better than Tinder for picking up women.

"I think that's your problem," Beau said.

"What's my problem?" Draper snapped. Beau's psychoanalysis was starting to get on his nerves.

"I think you have a hard time being alone."

"I don't."

Beau shrugged, but his expression looked as if he had something more to say. Draper didn't want to hear it.

"Okay. Enough. I get it," Draper said. "You think you're morally superior since you're settling down."

"I don't think that. Is it a crime to be happy and to want the same for my brother?"

"I'm genuinely happy for you and Sofia, Beau. But you need to understand that love isn't a one-size-fits-all thing. What's right for you may not be right for me."

"Understood. But if you're not serious about Ginny, I hope you won't lead her on and play the games you usually do with the women you date. Ginny is different. She's too nice to be treated that way."

Draper would never purposely hurt Ginny. It sickened him to think of causing her pain, but if he admitted this to his brother, Beau would use it as evidence to make his points that he hated to be alone and should consider settling down and recreating himself in the image of Beau.

Instead of defending himself, he focused on exorcising the strangely protective feelings for his neighbor this conversation had conjured.

In a silent standoff, Draper glared at Beau, who had pinned him with a steely gaze. It lasted a moment, as if they were in a staring contest and the first to blink was the loser.

But Draper was already feeling like the loser, because no matter how he tried to justify his time with Ginny, his brother was right. Draper had seen Ginny every day since the gala. He'd enjoyed her company, but he didn't want to give her the wrong idea.

Beau's phone rang. He picked it up and looked at it. "This is Josh. I need to take the call. He's got a quote for some work I want him to do on the house."

Beau answered the call. "Hey, Josh, thanks for getting back to me. Can you hold on a sec, I'm just leaving the office, but I need to tell Draper something before I go."

Beau stood.

"I have a meeting I need to get to." The tone of his voice was decidedly less hostile. "Are we okay here?"

Draper sat down at his desk and nodded.

"Yeah, we're fine. We're good. Go to your meeting."

After Beau left, Draper replayed the conversation in his head.

Where Ginny was concerned, he had simply intended it to be casual and neighborly. Well, except for the near kiss… And he supposed the expensive painting might have given the wrong impression…and the flowers, too. But when he saw them, he'd thought of how she loved to paint fresh flowers and— *Ugh.*

What had he done?

He really was an idiot not to realize how those gestures might have sent the wrong message.

He'd gotten caught up in the moment, wanting to help her embrace her talent.

But on that first day, Ginny had pointed out how giving Ines the Cartier bracelet would've been sending mixed signals.

Because he hadn't been serious about Ines. He simply liked to give nice gifts, which accounted for how he always found himself in the position of disengaging from women who wanted more emotionally than he could give them.

It might be a pattern.

The difference with Ginny was that none of the past women had lived next door.

Jerry's untimely arrival had been something close to divine intervention.

If Draper was going to start paying attention to signals, this was one he absolutely had to heed.

He needed to put a little neighborly distance between Ginny and himself. He knew just what he needed to do.

He pulled out his phone and scrolled until he got to recent calls. Then he tapped the screen.

"Hey, Natalie. It's Draper Fortune. Thanks for reaching out. Let's get that drink you suggested."

Saturday morning, Ginny looked out her bedroom window, down into Draper's driveway. His car was gone. It had been there last night.

Yes, she'd checked. She'd heard his car pull in around eight o'clock, and he hadn't gone out again. Ginny tried to convince herself it was a good thing that Draper was at home, seemingly alone, on the first night of the weekend, but she felt more confused than relieved because she hadn't seen him since Tuesday, when she'd staged the big unveiling of her art for him.

After seeing him five days in a row, she had gotten used to him knocking on the door.

When he didn't show Wednesday evening, Ginny had chalked it up to work or family or some other aspect of Draper's life that didn't involve her. Who knew, maybe he needed to do his laundry.

But when Thursday and Friday passed without a single word from him, she began to wonder if she had done something wrong or somehow offended him.

They'd almost kissed.

She'd thought she might've been mistaken about Saturday night after the gala, but Tuesday had left her with no doubt about Draper's intentions.

If not for Jerry barging in.

She sighed and stepped away from the window. It wasn't Jerry's fault. In hindsight, he had probably done her a favor by interrupting the kiss. The reality was, if Draper had really wanted to kiss her it would've happened. He could've come back Wednesday night or asked her out for the weekend. None of that happened.

So what was she supposed to think?

She felt like a caged animal hanging out in the house. So she laced on her running shoes and decided to go for a run to get out some of the excess energy that was making her want to climb the walls.

She ended up at Kirby's Perks, where her friend was working today. And while a Saturday morning at the coffee shop might not be the most private place to spill her guts, Ginny needed to talk to someone who could help her see things clearly.

"Maybe Jerry freaked him out?" Ginny whispered, leaning in so that Kirby could hear her over the buzz of the coffee-bean grinder. She cast a glance over her shoulder to see if any of the customers were listening.

Apparently not.

"Maybe he's been out of town on business?" Kirby suggested.

"No, he's been getting home late. Although, I guess it could be considered early for weekend standards. Anyway, his car was in the driveway when I went to bed last night, but it was gone again bright and early this morning." Ginny sighed. "I guess I was getting used to him coming over after he got home. It felt like we were establishing a pattern, but now, I miss him."

Kirby brewed the espresso and steamed the milk for two cappuccinos.

"If you miss him," she said, "what are you going to do about it?"

"What am I going to do about it?"

Searching for an answer, Ginny's gaze swept the coffee shop, landing on the wall where Kirby had displayed several of Ginny's framed watercolors. The collection included portraits of Lily and Violet, and one of Kirby behind the coffee bar. The rest were various landscapes. Even though they were vastly different from the florals she'd shown Draper on Tuesday, they made her think of him. Her heart twisted. Everywhere she looked she saw Draper and she had no idea what she was going to do about it.

When she finally chanced a glance back at Kirby, her friend leveled her with a look that suggested she wasn't going to let this go.

"Think about it while I deliver these drinks to table five. I'll be right back. And could you plate a strawberry muffin and deliver it to table ten?"

"Sure. Is Annette off today?"

Kirby grimaced. "No, she's running late."

Ginny was happy to help out, rather than slowing Kirby's Saturday roll.

Table ten was tucked in a corner and until Ginny approached with the muffin, she hadn't realized that

Honey from the Live and Let Dye salon was seated there, along with Lindy, the shop's hairstylist.

"Good morning, ladies," Ginny said. "Who ordered the strawberry muffin?"

Honey raised her hand. "Guilty as charged."

As Ginny set the plate in front of Honey, the two women exchanged a conspiratorial look.

"Thank you, baby girl," said Honey.

"You are very welcome. Let me know if you need anything else."

As Ginny turned to go back to the coffee bar, Honey said, "Are you working here again?"

"Oh, no, I just popped in for a coffee and I saw how busy the place is. You know how it is. You can't take the service out of a former server. I'm happy to help Kirby out."

"So I have a question for you," Honey said. "The other day when I was driving by your house, did I see you and that handsome Draper Fortune hanging out on your front porch?"

Ginny's face flamed. She steadied herself before she spoke, doing her best not to look guilty or lovestruck or...like an idiot for falling for a guy who was so not meant for her.

"Well, you know that Draper is my next-door neighbor, right? So it's not out of the question."

Perfect. At least it was better than trying to feign a puzzled "Draper who?"

"Well, y'all looked pretty cozy. You were drinking wine and it looked like there was some sort of to-do on your front porch. All kinds of signs set up on the porch or something."

"Oh! That must've been the day that Draper came over to see my art."

Ginny waved it away like it was nothing, even as she was inwardly kicking herself for not realizing that her front porch was tantamount to a stage in full view of the street. And, of course, one of the town's thirstiest busybodies would drive by when there was something juicy to see.

"That's right," Lindy said. "I forgot that you used to paint. Didn't we have an art class together in high school? That was so long ago, I can't really remember."

Ginny squinted at Lindy as if she was trying to recall, even though she knew they did. Lindy had graduated the year before Ginny, but in Lindy's senior year they'd been in class together.

"I think so," Ginny said.

"Well, that makes sense," Honey said. "It stands to reason that a wealthy man like him would want to look at art. Because I was having a tough time imagining the two of you together, if you know what I mean."

Honey laughed, but Ginny didn't.

"No. Exactly what do you mean?" Ginny asked.

Honey's smile faded. "Oh, no offense, hon. It's just that the women I've seen Draper with are glamorous. Not that you're not cute. She's very cute, isn't she, Lindy?"

Lindy nodded. “So cute. Adorable.”

Great. Just what she wanted to hear.

“Plus, doesn’t Draper have a girlfriend?” Honey said. “That woman from the celebrity gossip show?”

“Excuse me, Ginny,” said Kirby. “Can you help me with something in the kitchen? Annette just arrived and she can manage the counter. But I need some help lifting something.”

“Got to run,” Ginny said to Lindy and Honey as she telegraphed her most profound thanks to Kirby for rescuing her.

Once they were tucked away in the kitchen, Ginny said, “Honey saw Draper and me together on Wednesday. She had about a million questions.”

“What did you say?”

“I said he was my next-door neighbor, but she was fishing for a whole lot more than that because she’d zeroed in on the bottle of wine he brought over. I just wish things weren’t so up in the air.”

“You need to take matters into your own hands rather than sitting around and waiting for him to make the next move. Why don’t you offer to cook for him?”

Ginny grimaced.

“You’re a good cook, Ginny. If you want to make it less of a romantic dinner for two, why not invite him to Sunday dinner with your brothers. From what you said, it sounds like he and Jerry get along. Maybe Draper feels weird since Jerry walked in on the two of you. Sunday dinner would be a great way to break the ice.”

* * *

After Draper had a chance to process what Beau said about Ginny when he and his brother were in the office on Wednesday, Draper realized Beau was right. He didn't want to send Ginny the wrong message. Even though he enjoyed spending time with her, they were just friends.

If he hadn't been so weak in the moment and given in to his urge to kiss her—or almost kiss her, as had been the case—then it wouldn't matter. But he'd crossed that line and there was no going back now.

Ginny seemed serious by nature. She didn't seem the type of woman who indulged in casual flirting, much less casual flings. The bottom line was, he didn't know her well enough to be certain of what she wanted. Since he was attracted to her, but since he didn't want a serious relationship with anyone, he'd rather be safe than sorry.

He wasn't even sure he wanted to stay in Rambling Rose. He'd agreed to move here and help get the office up and running, but he hadn't signed on to live here forever. In fact, his heart was pretty set on moving back to New Orleans or somewhere else that wasn't quite so sleepy. Plus, there was the complication of being neighbors. There would be no escaping—for either of them—if something went wrong. And something always seemed to go wrong.

Yes. It was best for both of them to have some

breathing room so they could put things into perspective.

If he hadn't already figured that out, it might've seemed like a sign when Natalie Charles called to ask him out. Outside of work, Draper's favorite way to keep busy was spending time with a beautiful woman.

Draper had returned Natalie Charles's call with the intention of meeting her for that drink she had suggested, but she ended up inviting him to join her and a group of friends for some Saturday afternoon boating fun on Rambling Lake.

It turned out to be a beautiful sunny day. They'd had a nice time and it was low pressure since they were out as a group. As they docked, the lot of them decided to meet for dinner at Provisions.

Even though Draper would've preferred to call it a day, one of Natalie's friends, Jeff Edwards, the one with the boat, had recently come into some money and wanted Draper to give him some investment advice.

For that, Draper decided he could man up and join the group for dinner. Hell, he'd even buy Jeff's dinner. But it also meant that Natalie would come over to his house to shower and change rather than driving to her apartment in Austin and coming all the way back.

That Natalie happened to have a change of clothes suitable for a nice dinner out summed her up. She was fun, but she seemed the type who always had her eye out for an opportunity. Draper attracted the type like a magnet to a ball bearing. So, he'd already figured her out. He understood the value of *opportunities*, the difference was the ones he went after were business-oriented, not of the romantic nature.

Natalie sequestered herself in the guest bathroom off the hall, where he laid out fresh towels and a new bar of soap.

Draper retreated into the ensuite in his bedroom and proceeded to get ready.

He had just finished shaving and was standing in front of his closet with a towel wrapped around his waist when he heard the doorbell ring.

He considered not answering it, but his car was in the driveway.

He couldn't imagine who would be calling. Possibly Beau stopping by, as he did periodically.

Draper hopped on one foot as he pulled on his pants, then slipped into a white dress shirt, which he left open because the doorbell rang again and there was no time to button it.

Before he could get to the door, Natalie had answered it in what looked like some sort of towel with elastic that held it in place under her arms. It wasn't one of the towels he'd laid out for her. She must've brought her own. Her hair was wet and combed back from her face, but, remarkably, her makeup was perfect.

"It's for you," she said, shooting him a seductive look as she stepped away from the door to reveal Ginny standing there holding a book.

Her blue eyes looked huge. Twin patches of pink colored her cheeks. Her mouth was agape, but she remained quiet.

"Ginny, hi," Draper said as he did up a random button on his shirt. When she remained quiet, seemingly frozen in place, he stepped onto the porch and pulled the door closed behind him.

She looked so small and crestfallen. He was suddenly very aware how this must look to her—Natalie answering his door wearing that towel thing. Him coming up behind her with wet hair, barely dressed himself.

"Is everything okay?" he asked.

Why did he feel like he'd been caught cheating when he'd done absolutely nothing wrong?

That right there, that shadow of guilt, was exactly why dating his neighbor would never work. He couldn't promise Ginny anything exclusive, yet situations like this were bound to happen and they would always be awkward.

"I'm sorry," Ginny finally said. "I didn't realize you had company."

"I don't have company. Not really."

She frowned and it scrunched her nose and curled her upper lip.

"You don't owe me an explanation, Draper. I'll let you get back to her."

She took a step back.

"Wait. Are you okay?" he asked.

"I'm fine," she said, but she didn't sound fine.

He knew he should just let her go, but he asked, “Is that for me?” He nodded at the book in her hands.

She glanced down as if she’d forgotten what she was carrying.

“Oh. Yes. Well, I just stopped by to lend you *Wuthering Heights*. I forgot to give it to you when you were over Tuesday.”

She handed it to him and turned to go.

“Ginny, wait.”

But she kept walking.

Chapter Eight

It was the woman from the gala.

Natalie McFlirty. Or whatever her last name was.

She was the woman in the towel in Draper's house.

Ginny spent the rest of Saturday night trying to convince herself she didn't care, but she couldn't quite make her heart believe it.

Even though she knew she had no right to feel upset, she did.

She did. There. She'd finally admitted it. Wasn't acknowledgement the first step toward getting over hurt?

Acknowledgement and no longer looking out the window to see if Draper's car was in the driveway. She was done with that.

Just as right now, as she stood in the kitchen making the lasagna for tonight's family dinner, she had no idea whether Draper was home or out—alone or had company.

Nope. Not her concern.

Even if she still was grousing over the situation, trying to make sense of it.

This morning, she wasn't quite as angry as she'd been yesterday, but she still had so many questions. Such as, was that how Draper operated? Even if the gala hadn't been a proper date, it felt disrespectful for him to pick up other women while he was out with her. But how did they get in touch with each other? When did he have time to get her number?

She layered another round of noodles, meat sauce and cheese.

She and Draper had been together all night except for a couple of trips to the ladies room and the short time she had danced with Linton Nash, which, she supposed, could've been viewed as a similar transgression—but, no, it wasn't really.

The guy had cut in while they were dancing. It had been one short, rather fast-tempo song and then she had met Draper back at the table. Had he worked so fast that he was able to find Natalie, get her number and get back to the table before she left the dance floor?

She had no idea if Draper's faster, more glamorous crowd played by different rules than she was used to. Clearly, she wasn't good at navigating his world.

Whatever.

Ginny wished she could put it out of her mind. She had obviously mistaken Draper's intent. Her bad.

Ugh, but taking him a classic novel on a Saturday night? Why had she thought that was a good idea? She should have just invited him over to sit on the front porch swing, knit a scarf and sip sweet tea.

Oh, right, she'd already wowed him with two out of three of those thrillers.

Was it any wonder he was out with McFlirty?

As she opened the oven door and slid the lasagna onto the middle rack, Jerry walked into the kitchen.

"Something smells good," he said. "What time are we eating?"

"The lasagna takes about a half hour to bake. Any time after that, as long as Scott and Dane are here."

"What about Fortune? Is he still coming over?" Jerry asked.

"He's not." The words stung the back of her throat and made her eyes burn. She busied herself at the sink, rinsing the lettuce for their salad.

"I thought you were inviting him."

If she could've kicked herself for sharing that tidbit with Jerry—with all three of her brothers, for that matter—she would've done it. Why had she told them?

Why? Since Sunday night was usually family

night, she thought she owed it to them to ask if they minded if she invited a guest.

"Did you change your mind?" Jerry asked.

"Yep." She knew her clipped words were a dead giveaway that she was upset, and she was trying so hard not to be.

But she was and she couldn't help it. She felt like if she said too much, the dam that was holding back her emotions might break and she would start crying.

"Hey, are you okay?" Jerry walked up and put a hand on her shoulder. She shrugged him off under the pretense of needing to turn off the water.

"Okay. You are definitely upset," Jerry said.

"Who's upset?" Scott asked as he and Dane entered the kitchen.

Shoot. Shoot. She felt her eyes welling up.

"Nobody is upset," Ginny snapped. "Though it would be nice to get a little help in the kitchen for a change."

She slammed the metal colander with the lettuce down on the granite counter, then brushed past her brothers and raced up the stairs as the tears started falling.

She locked herself in the bathroom, where she splashed water on her face until she got herself together.

"What is wrong with you?" she asked as she looked at herself in the mirror. Of course, it could be taken two ways: what was so wrong with her that Draper Fortune was taking a pass? Or what was wrong with her that she would think that one date that wasn't even a date, and three subsequent visits and an art swap meant there was something between her and Draper?

"He almost kissed me," she murmured. "And I almost let him."

She hadn't let anyone that close since… Trey Hartnet.

Even thinking the name made her shiver.

But he had no power over her. Her therapist had helped her see that… unless she gave him that power. She was in control of the situation.

The same went for Draper Fortune, who, despite his wandering eye, was a much better man than Trey Hartnet. At least he didn't hurt women. Not physically, anyway.

Well, he wouldn't get the chance to hurt her emotionally, and—

"Trey Hartnet." She said his name aloud, looked herself square in the eyes in the mirror and straightened her shoulders. "You have no power over me."

She reapplied her mascara, brushed her hair and went downstairs.

It was about time to take the lasagna out of the oven. In the midst of everything, she had forgotten to set a timer. She'd cooked this recipe so often—it was her brothers' favorite—that she could eyeball it and tell if it was done.

By the time she reached the kitchen, the table was set, the salad had been made and served on four small plates, the bread was sliced and in a basket. Scott was opening a bottle of red wine.

They all glanced at her and then at each other as if they were taking an atmospheric reading before they dared to utter a word.

Ginny took the lead. "Thank you for doing all this." She swept her hand toward the table. She knew it was their way of making her feel better and she loved them for it. Even if things didn't work out in the dating department, at least she knew she had three men—four, if she counted her father—she could always count on. "The lasagna should be done. Let me get it out of the oven and we'll be ready to sit down."

The guys shuffled around the kitchen, making corny jokes that Ginny was sure were for her benefit, as she sliced and plated the lasagna. Each brother grabbed one serving as it was ready, then they finally sat down at the table.

A heavy silence hung over them, until Scott finally said, "Are you okay?"

Even before she looked up from her plate, she felt the piercing gazes of her three brothers.

"I'm fine," Ginny said. Before she could think better of it, she forked a steaming bite into her mouth and started chewing. The hot bite felt like it blistered the top of her mouth, making her eyes water. She grabbed her wine and took a long drink.

"You don't seem fine," Dane said.

"No, you don't," Scott said.

"I just scalded the roof of my mouth," she said.

Scott continued, "Do we need to have a talk with Draper Fortune?"

She took another gulp of wine and it went down the wrong pipe, causing her to choke. When she'd finished coughing, she shot Jerry a how-could-you look. The only way Dane and Scott would've known was if Jerry had spilled the beans.

"What?" Jerry gave her a wide-eyed, palms-up shrug.

"You have a big mouth," she said to him and then turned to Dane and Scott. "No one in this room needs to say a word to Draper Fortune."

"You're in this room," Dane said. "So I guess that includes you."

Ginny rolled her eyes at him.

"Seriously, Ginny," said Scott. "The guy is bad news. You'd be smart to stay away from him."

"What do you mean, he's bad news?" she asked. "You don't even know him."

"I know that he has a reputation for being a first class womanizer."

"I guess it takes one to know one." Dane laughed at his own joke, but sobered when he realized none of his siblings were laughing with him. He bowed his head and turned his attention to the piece of bread he was now buttering with painstaking precision.

"As I was saying," Scott continued. "If I'd known you were interested in him, I would've warned you sooner."

"I'm not interested in him," Ginny said.

Not anymore.

She knew her brothers meant well, but the last thing she needed right now was for them to gang up on Draper on her behalf. Because that would mean she cared, that he mattered.

And he didn't.

Not anymore.

"I don't know anything about Fortune's love life and frankly, I don't care," Jerry said. "Every time I've seen the two of them together he's always acted like a gentleman. Plus, the guy is pretty well connected and he seems mostly interested in Ginny's art."

In spite of herself, Ginny's heart sank. So she really had been reading more into this than was there. At least she thought that until Jerry looked at her and seemed to telegraph a silent addendum: *Except for that last night when I walked in just before he was going to kiss you.*

Feeling her cheeks warm, Ginny looked away and then surreptitiously glanced at Dane and Scott to see if they'd picked up on her reaction.

Apparently not.

"Fortune has been encouraging her and he's even promised to introduce her to a gallery owner from New Orleans—I guess that's where he's from. Or at least that's what Ginny said." Jerry glanced at her and paused, as if she was supposed to pick up the story. When Ginny said nothing, he went on. "Even if Ginny's not interested in dating him, she needs to hold him to that promise. Otherwise, she's letting an opportunity slip through her fingers. Right?"

She met him with a blank stare, but he continued, "Tell them about this woman he wants you to meet, Gin."

On New Year's Eve, when Ginny had confided her discontent to Jerry, she had asked him to make sure she stuck to her vow to paint and make changes for the better. At the time, she had no idea that Draper Fortune would factor into the equation.

"I don't know," she said. "I don't even know if I want to go. I mean, she's based in New Orleans. I'm here. What good is it?"

"What good is it?" Jerry was incredulous. "It's a great opportunity. Most artists are in galleries that aren't in their hometowns. Especially when their hometown doesn't even have a fine art gallery. Look, you told me to hold you accountable and that's what I'm doing. You need to seize this opportunity to meet that gallery owner and then find a way to get involved in the Austin art scene."

He was right, but given her past, stepping out of her comfort zone was a big deal. Of course, her brothers had no idea what happened. So, how were they supposed to know?

Monday morning, as Draper was getting into his car to go to work, he heard the sound of someone rolling a garbage can toward the curb. It was coming from the other side of the fence. His gut clenched. He hadn't talked to Ginny since she'd brought over the book on Saturday. He'd been at a loss for words then and even now, faced with the possibility of meeting her at the street as they both set out the garbage, he wasn't sure what to say. Should he apologize or try to explain?

He'd gotten back from the dinner with Natalie and her friends relatively early. The night had turned out to be a disaster. After he'd pushed Natalie's friend, Jeff Edwards, about committing to an appointment to come into the office to discuss investment opportunities, it had finally come out that he had already spent most of his inherited money on a Maserati, the boat on which they'd partied on Saturday and a house in Rambling Rose Estates. All the talk about investments when they'd been on the boat had been to impress his date.

That night at the restaurant, he'd pulled Draper aside and fessed up.

After that, Natalie had too much to drink and wanted to spend the night at Draper's house rather than going home. He wasn't about to sleep with a drunk woman. But he certainly couldn't let her drive home, nor did he feel right about putting her in an Uber. So he drove her home. By the time he made sure she was safely inside her apartment, she was a blubbering, sobbing mess, asking him why he was rejecting her and what was wrong with her that made men never fell in love with her.

Draper couldn't get away fast enough.

He had gotten home by ten thirty on Saturday night and had spent Sunday alone doing a lot of soul-searching.

He was so tired of attracting women who brought the drama, which made him appreciate Ginny's sweet, quiet way even more. Could he blame her for walking away after a strange woman answered his door in a towel? And shouldn't that have been his first clue that Natalie was trouble?

He wanted to talk to Ginny. But what should he say?

That was just one of the questions bouncing around his head and keeping him awake all weekend.

By 4:30 a.m. on Monday, he decided it was better to get up and do something productive. And, yes, it crossed his mind that if he was outside getting in his car around 5:45 a.m., he might casually run in to Ginny.

So when he heard the sound of the rolling garbage can on the other side of the hedge, he grabbed his own garbage can and began trekking toward the curb with a smile and a knot in his stomach.

"Good morning," he said.

His stomach dipped in disappointment when Ginny's brother Jerry stepped out from behind the hedge and rolled the can out onto the sidewalk.

"Morning," Jerry murmured. Draper wasn't sure if he wasn't a morning person or if he was pissed off on his sister's behalf.

"How's Ginny?" Draper asked before he could think better of it.

"She's..." Jerry narrowed his eyes as if weighing his words. "She's fine. She's looking forward to meeting your friend who owns that gallery in New Orleans. That's this weekend, isn't it?"

"It is," Draper said.

"Good." Jerry nodded, but he didn't look very agreeable.

Draper nodded. This was good. If her brother was on board it meant Draper might have a chance...for what, he wasn't quite sure.

A chance to see her again and explain that Natalie was a mistake... No, that made her seem too important, like he'd been interested in her. That Natalie had called him and then come on like a hurricane? No, that made him seem weak.

Well, he didn't have to figure it out just yet. But he would.

"Then you're going to call her and fill her in on the details?" Jerry said.

"Absolutely. Wait, I don't have her number. Could you please give it to me?"

Jerry looked at him, unsmiling, as if he was sizing up Draper. Then he held out his hand. "Give me your phone."

Draper fished in his pocket, typed in the access code and handed the phone to Jerry with the contact app open.

Jerry clicked around a bit and then pressed the phone up to his ear.

"Hey, Gin, it's Jerry. I'm calling from Draper Fortune's phone."

He was silent for a moment and Draper could hear the sound of Ginny's voice in the still of the morning, but he couldn't make out exactly what she was saying.

"No. No, everything is fine," Jerry finally said. "I just put your number in his phone. He's going to call you later and give you details about meeting his gallery friend."

She was saying something that didn't sound completely happy when Jerry said, "Gotta go. 'Bye." And he disconnected the call.

As he handed the phone back to Draper, he said, "She's expecting your call. I know I can count on you not to let her down."

Draper waited until three o'clock to call Ginny. He remembered her mentioning that the last bell rang at two thirty. He wanted to give her enough time for the kids to clear the classroom.

He figured that was the earliest he should call.

Sitting at his desk in the Fortune Investments office, he pushed the call button and sat back in his chair, staring at the corner of the ceiling as it rang once, twice...three times. In his head, he began composing the message he'd leave on her voice mail, when she finally answered.

"Hello?"

The sound of her voice made him suck in a breath.

"Hi, Ginny," he said. "It's Draper."

She was quiet for a beat, and just as he started to wonder if the call had gotten dropped—or worse, if she'd hung up on him—she said, "Hi, Draper."

The sound of her saying his name did something strange to his stomach.

"Hi, um, yeah, I was just calling to make sure we're still on for Saturday night."

Again, there was silence on her end.

In the void, he wondered if he should try to explain the Natalie situation, but she answered before he could.

"I don't know," she said. "Can you tell me more about it?"

Oh. Okay. It wasn't a definite no.

"My friend Mackenzie Cole will be in Austin this weekend. The Museum of Women in the Arts is honoring her for her work."

Silence.

"I hate to subject you to yet another stuffy black-tie dinner, but I can assure you it'll be worth the pomp. Macks is great. She's someone you need to know, and I know she's going to love your work. In fact, right after we get off the phone, I'm going to send her pictures of the pieces I have."

He stopped at that, deciding to employ an old trick he'd learned in sales—be quiet until the other person speaks.

"Is that what you do in your free time?" she asked. "Go to black-tie events?"

Her reply disarmed him, and he laughed. "It must seem like it, right? But look, as I said, Macks is someone you really need to know. She's a great champion of women in the arts."

"Hence the award," Ginny said.

"What?"

"Her award for her efforts supporting women in the arts."

"Right. Right," Draper answered.

Ginny sighed and it made him think of how her breath had smelled like the berry notes of the wine they'd been drinking right before he'd almost kissed her.

He squeezed his eyes shut and opened them again, as if he could clear away the thought.

"Could I meet her on Sunday?"

"That's not going to work because she's leaving early Sunday morning."

"Look, um, I appreciate you thinking of me, Draper," she said. "I know you're just trying to help me and I don't want to seem ungrateful, but I'm going to be real with you. I don't have anything appropriate to wear to a black-tie event. I borrowed the dress I wore to the Austin Arts Gala and I'm fresh out of options."

Draper sat up in his chair, and a smile spread over his face. "If that's your only hesitation, it's an easy fix. In fact, what are you doing right now?"

* * *

From the front porch, Ginny watched Draper's car pull into her driveway.

As he hopped out and headed toward her house, Ginny felt that familiar churn of anticipation. He was here. Seeing him walk toward her felt like falling backward into a feather bed. There was that sensation of dropping, but also that split second of weightless wonder before touching down.

"Are you ready?" he called.

"I think so," she said as she walked down the steps toward him. "Where are we going?"

When she got home, she had changed from her jeans and T-shirt into a sundress. It wasn't fancy, but what sort of swanky outing could be happening at four o'clock on a Monday afternoon? Surely, this wasn't another black-tie surprise.

"I have a friend who is just starting out as a fashion designer in Austin," Draper said.

Understanding dropped like lead in her chest.

I can't afford to buy a designer gown that I'll wear once at an event I'm not even comfortable attending.

As if he'd read her mind, Draper said, "You'll be doing her a favor wearing one of her dresses. The women at the event will see it on you and flock to her shop to buy her clothes. It's a win-win. A dress for you to wear and a walking advertisement for her."

At five foot two, Ginny knew she was hardly model material, but maybe it would be a chance to show how this designer's clothing looked on regular women.

"What's her name?" Ginny asked.

"Anna Ferguson."

"Another old girlfriend?" She hadn't meant to say that out loud. Or maybe she had. She wanted to know.

"No, Anna is just someone I know."

Someone you want to date?

Ginny pulled in her lips and bit down. That was none of her business and she shouldn't care. But…

"Okay, full disclosure," Draper said. "I went out with her twin sister a couple of times and now we're all friends."

"Is there anyone in Central Texas you haven't dated?"

He laughed. When he slanted a quick glance at her, she could see he wasn't offended. That was good. She hadn't wanted to offend him. What she meant was that she and Draper really did live in different worlds.

Not that one was better than the other. Though his certainly was more glamorous.

She studied his profile as he drove. She didn't want to pretend to be someone she wasn't, but maybe she could learn a thing or two from him about lightening up and going where life led.

"All right, look," he said. "That woman, Natalie, who answered my door Saturday—"

"Draper, you don't owe me an explanation."

"But I feel like I do. I want to give you an explanation."

He did? Her stomach flipped and bunched.

"Do you remember her from the Austin Arts Gala?" he asked.

For a second, Ginny wanted to say no, she didn't remember her. Because recognizing McFlirty would mean that she cared and she shouldn't, but…

"Yes, she checked us in when we arrived."

The truth was always the best policy.

"She got my number from the gala registration records and called me. We went out Saturday, but it was a disaster."

Why was she answering your door in a towel?

"I'm sorry it didn't work out," Ginny said. She meant to leave it there, but then added, "Was her towel not suitable attire for your date?"

Ugh. Ugh, ugh, ugh. Why did she say that?

Well, she had and now she had to own it.

"Yeah, about that." Draper stopped at a red light and looked at Ginny. "Earlier Saturday, we went out on a boat with some of her friends."

He explained the events that followed: from her wanting to shower and change at his house, to the business that he thought he was courting evaporating, to Natalie's subsequent meltdown.

"Wow," Ginny said. "That does sound like a disaster. Draper, where do you find these women?"

He laughed. It was a true belly laugh, which had her laughing, too.

"I have no idea," he said. "But I really do need to be more discerning, don't I?"

Draper was looking straight ahead when he said that, not at her. When the light turned green and he accelerated through the intersection, the air felt lighter even with the spark of electricity that seemed to be zinging back and forth between them.

The boutique was located in the trendy 2nd Street District.

Anna, a willowy blonde with a nose ring and a tattoo on the inside of her wrist, looked more boho chic than gala elegant. She greeted both of them warmly with kisses on both cheeks. Ginny felt no residual awkwardness over Draper having dated Anna's twin sister, nor any passive-aggressive, you-might-think-you-have-him-but-watch-me-take-him-away-from-you posturing.

As Anna ushered Ginny back to a fitting room, she said, "I've set aside several dresses for you to choose from. Let me know if you need help with zippers or hooks."

"Thank you so much for doing this, Anna," Ginny said. "I really appreciate you lending me a dress."

The woman's blue eyes sparkled. "I'm the one who should be thanking you. I'm so excited that you want to wear one of my designs to the event. Will you tag me in all the photos you post?"

Because she was a teacher, Ginny wasn't active on social media. Not that anything she might post would be scandalous or unfit for children, but she didn't think it was necessary to post about her life outside of the classroom.

However, it might be time for Ginny the artist to consider posting her work. After all, she had encouraged the students in her art club to use Instagram like their own personal galleries.

Since she was going to an art-related event and Anna was being so wonderful to lend her the dress, it was the least she could do.

"Absolutely," Ginny said.

"Before you leave, I'll give you a card with all my socials on it," Anna said. "But be sure to come out and show us each dress as you try them on. I want to see all of them."

Each dress was pretty in its own way. Not all of them were her style, though Ginny would be hard-pressed to articulate her style. She knew what she liked when she saw it. Most of the time that depended on how the clothing felt on her body. It could be the most gorgeous dress, but if it didn't feel good, she wasn't about to spend the evening tugging at her outfit.

That's why when she slipped into the gorgeous multicolored halter dress with the hammered silver choker, she knew it was perfect. The silky fabric whispered over her skin, hitting her in all the right places. This was a dress that made her spin around in the fitting room, admire it from every angle and say "Wow." Because even Ginny had to admit, the transformation was stunning.

On their way to the shop, if she thought she might have imagined that something had shifted between her and Draper, the look on his face when she walked out of the fitting room confirmed it now. Suddenly, the air seemed different between them.

She stood taller, with her shoulders back.

“Wow is right,” Draper said. “You look beautiful.”

For the first time in a long time, she felt beautiful.

“The exhibit I’m planning will feature unknown women artists across America,” Mackenzie Cole, or Macks, as she insisted on being called, told Ginny on Saturday night after the awards ceremony. “I think your work would fit in perfectly.”

Ginny was so struck by how Macks was a doppelgänger for the actress Margot Robbie that she almost missed the woman explaining that the artist from Texas that she’d originally secured for the show had withdrawn because of a family crisis. When she’d asked Draper if he knew of anyone from the area he would recommend—someone fresh, a new perspective—he’d sent her a photo of Ginny’s work.

And the rest was history. Or it would be.

Right now, in the moment, Ginny felt like Cinderella again. Only this time she wasn’t afraid that her dress would turn into rags.

Was it the gown? Or the fact that Macks loved Ginny’s artistic style?

Or the way Draper was looking at her?

Maybe a combination of all three.

There was no denying that tonight Draper seemed extra attentive.

And Macks, who could've chosen any artist in Texas, was giving Ginny the opportunity of a lifetime. Or at least that's how it felt.

"The show is at my gallery in New Orleans," Macks continued. "It's only a couple of weeks away, but I'd love to show one of the pieces Draper sent to me—the one with the pink and white flowers in the blue vase. That is, if I can get him to part with it temporarily."

Draper made noises pretending to think about it, but he was joking.

"Then you choose two more that you think will complement that one," Macks told her.

The night ended too soon. On the drive back to Rambling Rose, Ginny and Draper talked easily about the upcoming show.

"You're going to New Orleans for it, aren't you?" he asked.

When she hesitated, he said, "You have to go, Ginny. You can't miss your first show."

"I wish I could. But I don't think I can swing it. It's happening about a month before school gets out. It'll be hard for me to get away."

"What are you talking about? You don't teach on the weekend. Go for the show and come back."

"I wish, but it's longer than a seven-hour drive. It would be too rushed."

What she didn't want to say was that she didn't

trust her old car to make the trip. Because it would feel like she was fishing for Draper to come to her rescue, as he had with everything since they'd met.

"We're not going to spoil an otherwise perfect night by talking about that, even though I have no intention of letting it go. Only for now. But you know what this occasion is missing?"

"What?"

He put on his turn signal and steered his Tesla to a liquor store, where he bought a bottle of champagne.

When they got back to his house, they took the bottle out to the back porch, under the market lights he'd strung up, and toasted her good news.

Draper touched his glass to hers. "Here's to the first of many good things."

"And here's to you for making things happen."

The lights brought out flecks of amber in his eyes and those eyes were on her. Her gaze fell to his lips. Oh, those delicious, inviting lips. They were so tempting and they were just a breath away from hers.

Feeling beautiful in her dress, and high on promise and bubbly, Ginny closed her eyes and Draper leaned in and kissed her.

His kiss was surprisingly gentle.

Just the whisper of lips.

So tender, it made her crave more.

Her lips opened under his and she invited him in, letting passion take over. For a moment she lost herself in the closeness, in the feel of him, his lips on hers, moving from her mouth to that sensitive spot at the base of her ear. His hands on her bare back. His fingers slipping between the fabric of the halter dress to caress the bare skin hidden inside.

She hasn't kissed a man in so long.

Since *that night* all those years ago.

When his hands were on her.

Pushing at her clothes, pawing at her.

When he kept demanding more and more.

She'd said no. And she'd meant no. But he wouldn't stop—

"Stop! No!"

Ginny shoved him away and stumbled backward to the sound of glass shattering.

Disoriented, she blinked, up at the market lights then down at the broken glass at her feet.

"Ginny?" Draper tried to touch her arm, but she jerked back, away from his touch.

But it was Draper, not Trey.

Her hand flew to her mouth, muffling her sobs.

Like Cinderella at midnight, all she could do was run away.

Chapter Nine

Sunday morning, Draper was driving home from Kirby's Perks, where he'd picked up coffee and an assortment of muffins when he passed Ginny's house and saw her putting something into the trunk of her car.

He parked in his driveway, jumped out and rounded the hedge just as she was unlocking her door. Something had spooked her last night when they'd kissed. At first she'd seemed to be into it, but then it was as if a switch had flipped and she was experiencing some sort of flashback. Even though he should leave this alone, let her be, he knew he wasn't going to be able to just forget it. He needed to figure out what he had done, without frightening her again.

The light of day, when neither of them had been drinking, neither of them had over imbibed, was the perfect time. Draper hated getting drunk. Drunk led to sloppy and out of control.

When you were out of control, that's when things happened to you instead of you being in control of your world. His brother Austin didn't have a problem with alcohol, but when he'd lost control of his situation, that was when the con artist who would become his first wife had swooped in and took him for a ride.

Draper had promised himself that would never happen to him. To keep that promise, he needed to be in control. Always.

"Good morning," he said as he rounded the hedge.

Ginny was wearing a tank top, and jeans tucked into riding boots. Her long brown hair was pulled back into one of those fancy braids that laced down the back of her head. He thought he remembered his sister calling it a French braid. Maybe not. But that wasn't important right now.

Ginny looked up at him with a neutral expression—neither smiling nor frowning. Her eyes were covered with sunglasses so he couldn't see them to get a read.

"Hey, Draper," she said.

But that was all she said.

"I had a good time last night," he said and cringed, fearing it was the wrong thing to say.

Maybe it was because she didn't answer him.

"Hey, look, I just came over to see if you were okay. You left sort of suddenly last night."

Again, she didn't say anything.

"I just— I hope I didn't do something wrong. I've been trying to figure it out and all I can come up with is the kiss. If I was out of line, I'm sorry."

He saw her let out a breath that seemed to relax her entire body.

"It's not your fault," she said. "It's..." She sighed. "It's a long story and I can't get into it right now. But thanks for last night. Thanks for introducing me to Macks and for everything. I need to run."

"Where are you going?" he asked.

She put her hand on the top of the open driver's side door of her blue Honda.

"I'm heading out to the stables to ride."

"You ride?" he said. "I had no idea that you rode. I love horses. Maybe someday you can show me around the stables."

He was telling the truth. He'd learned to ride when he was growing up and he did love horses. The only problem was he hadn't ridden since he was in middle school. He'd just wanted to keep her talking because maybe then he could get to the bottom of what had made her run last night.

"But I just wanted you to know I'm sorry if I overstepped last night," he said. "I hope it won't affect our friendship."

"Draper, of course, it won't. It's not you, it's me. I'm just not sure this is the best time for me to get into a relationship."

Wow. That was a switch. Usually he was the one

giving that speech and his dates were doing their best to make him stay.

"I appreciate you apologizing, but everything is fine."

She started to slide into the car, but she stopped and turned back to him.

"If you're not doing anything this morning, would you like to go riding with me?"

Ginny wasn't sure what horrified her more: that she'd lost control and allowed Draper to kiss her, or that she'd freaked out and run away after he did.

When she'd gotten in last night, she'd glimpsed herself in the foyer mirror. Her pretty dress and tearstained face were a strange juxtaposition that seemed more like a nightmare than a fairy tale.

Draper probably thought she was a freak. And with good reason. Because why wouldn't he, when the woman he'd kissed cried and bolted.

She'd tossed and turned all night, wallowing in her humiliation, until she'd finally dragged herself out of bed with the determination to get out of the house, get away from his presence next door and clear her head.

The best way to do that was to go riding.

An old high school friend still lived on his family's ranch on the outskirts of Rambling Rose. He'd told her she was welcome to come out and saddle up any time she wanted. It had been a while since she'd been out there, but she couldn't think of anything else she'd rather do today.

Well, except for possibly hitting a universal rewind button and redoing last night's ungraceful grand finale.

She had been both mortified and relieved when Draper had shown up and wanted to talk.

Before they left, he'd gone inside to change into jeans and tennis shoes. He'd invited her to come in, but she'd opted to stay outside. The cool April morning air was doing wonders to clear her head.

Draper finally reappeared with a couple of muffins and two coffees in to-go cups.

"I ran to Kirby's Perks this morning and I grabbed a breakfast. If I'd known I would be running into you, I would've picked up two coffees." He shrugged. "I brewed you some when I was inside. Gotta love the magic of a Keurig. I would've made you a cappuccino, but I didn't want to keep you waiting."

Despite his occasional cluelessness that sometimes gave women the wrong idea, the man had such a good heart and generous spirit.

Now, as she drove them to the Wild Rose Ranch, it sort of felt like a...well, it wasn't exactly a *do-over* as much as it was a chance to show him that she wasn't a total freak.

Out on the trail, Ginny could finally breathe. She didn't have to worry about who was judging her or what she was wearing. She felt free. Draper seemed to be enjoying himself, too.

At first, they rode together without much conversation. Even in the silence, out on the decidedly unglamorous trails that wound through the Wild Rose Ranch, Draper seemed relaxed. If he was put off by what had happened last night, he wasn't letting it show.

When the trail opened up to a meadow, Ginny coaxed her bay quarter horse into a run. Draper followed without hesitation.

When they slowed, Ginny said, "I wasn't sure what kind of a horseman you'd be."

He smiled. "Was that sprint a test?"

"Maybe." She laughed and tucked a piece of hair that the wind had blown into her face behind her ear. "You passed."

"That's good to know."

Their light banter lifted the trace of tension from Ginny's shoulders. She was so grateful that she hadn't ruined things between them. She was grateful that Draper was the kind of man who could look beyond human foibles and not permanently brand a person.

They came to a creek on the outer edge of the meadow and decided to let the horses get a drink of water and rest. The two of them dismounted and walked over to a shady spot under a pecan tree.

Just as easily as they'd ridden in companionable silence, they shifted into effortless conversation.

Draper expanded on what he'd told her that first day, when they'd had coffee after Ines had thrown the candy in her yard—Ginny smiled as she made a mental note to thank Ines someday—about his idyllic childhood growing up in New Orleans as part of a large, loving, close-knit family.

"My parents are the best," he said. "They raised me to believe I could do anything."

"That's great," she said. "Family is everything to me. My brothers and I are super close."

Draper chuckled. "I had a feeling you were."

"What do you mean?"

Draper looked a little sheepish. "That morning that I got your number from Jerry…let's just say that he seemed protective."

"That's a hazard of being a little sister to three brothers. And something that any guy who tries to get close to their baby sister has to face."

She hadn't really meant to edge the conversation into romantic territory, but it sort of led itself there.

"Is that what we're doing, Ginny? Are we getting closer?"

She knew it was a veiled reference to what happened last night.

She wasn't quite sure how to respond.

"Do you want to talk about last night?" he said.

She did.

It surprised her, but she really did want to talk about it. Maybe it would be the first step toward getting over it, trying to keep it buried, as she had all these years.

"Out of sight, out of mind" obviously didn't mean it was out of her subconscious or that she had learned how to cope with it. She'd simply been ignoring the specter of Trey Hartnet that had been terrorizing her for nearly a decade.

"So, where to start?" Her heart was thudding in her chest. For a moment, she felt like she couldn't breathe. But she inhaled a slow, deep breath and exhaled for a longer, slower count. Just as her counselor had taught her to do when she felt overwhelmed.

"Start from the beginning?" Draper suggested.

She nodded.

"My parents…my parents are great. Smart and loving, but they were strict, and, like I said, I grew up with three *über*-protective older brothers. So you might say I was somewhat sheltered growing up. I've had one long-term boyfriend. We dated seriously all through high school, but we got accepted to different colleges. So we decided to take a break while we were away and revisit things after graduation. You know, if we were still in love, we would get back together and get engaged. Sounds reasonable, right?

"As many first loves go, he found someone else. So during the spring term of my freshman year, I was a free agent. My friends tried really hard to convince me that I needed to make up for lost time. This guy named Trey—he was in my studio painting class back when I was still an art major—bonded with me and we used to spend hours in the studio painting. Sometimes we'd be there until the sun was coming up. I thought it was great. I had this guy friend who was there with me. I felt so safe. He would make me laugh and we'd joke around. It was fun to have a guy friend to go out dancing with or to parties. Sometimes we'd go out with a big group of friends. Sometimes it was just us. It wasn't anything romantic. We were just hanging out like college kids do.

"The week before finals, we went to a party and he was walking me home, like he'd been doing for weeks, but he said he needed to stop by the studio and get something. It was after two in the morning. We were the only people there. He went into this storage closet in the back of the room and asked me if I could help him with something. I didn't think anything of it…but he blocked the door and he wouldn't let me out—"

Her voice caught and the words logjammed in the back of her throat, damming up the scalding bile until she had tears in her eyes. For a moment, the old familiar fight-or-flight feeling engulfed her like a hood blinding her to everything else but her fears.

Not this time, she told herself.

She had been running from what Trey Hartnet had done to her for too long.

"He hurt you." It wasn't a question. Draper's voice was a low growl.

She nodded and felt the tears fall from her eyes, spilling onto her cheeks.

"He said that I'd been sending him signals all semester that I wanted it just as bad as he did. But I didn't. He was my friend."

"Did you tell anyone?"

She shook her head and buried her face in her hands. "He said no one would believe me. Since I'd been drinking and people saw how I'd been all over him at the party. It wasn't true, but he was like Dr. Jekyll and Mr. Hyde. One minute he was my best friend, then all of a sudden he was…a monster.

"I kind of fell apart after that. I left school. I didn't even take my finals. I came home claiming I was sick. It wasn't a lie. I was so disgusted that I couldn't even look at myself in the mirror."

"I'm so sorry he did that to you." Draper made that low, growling sound again and then smacked his right fist into his left hand. "I wish I could get ahold of that bastard. I'd teach him that no means no."

As if moved by a force beyond her, Ginny reached out and touched Draper's arm.

"I'm sorry," he said. "That just makes me so mad. I didn't know you in college, but I know you now and you are the kindest, gentlest woman I've met. That someone could take advantage of that kindness makes me—"

He swallowed hard, and Ginny saw the tears glistening in his eyes.

"I'm so sorry," he whispered.

He took her hand in his and laced their fingers together. Ginny had no idea how much time passed as they sat there holding hands.

But it was nice. It was…healing.

Finally, he asked, "What happened with school?"

She grimaced. "All of my teachers except for one gave me an incomplete until I could come in and make up the final. The one that failed me was the studio art professor."

A hiccup of a laugh escaped from her throat.

"Ironic, huh?" she said. "Well, it was just as well. I had a hard enough time making myself go back to school. For a long time that summer, I had made up my mind to stay here and go to community college rather than going back. But after I had a chance to think about it, I went back and took the makeup exams, and decided I wasn't going to let Trey take that away from me, too. The campus was big enough that if I changed my major, I thought I could avoid running into him." She shrugged.

"Did you ever see him again?"

She shook her head. "One of my friends who used to hang out in the same group said that Trey didn't come back to school that next fall. There was speculation that he might have failed out. I didn't really care. Since he wasn't there, at least I didn't have to explain. But I still felt like I had to look over my shoulder. Sometimes on campus, I'd catch a glimpse of someone with his build or blond curly hair like he had and I'd go into a tailspin. But the problem was, I couldn't tell anyone what happened. I was too ashamed. For the most part, I had complete tunnel vision and focused on school. I didn't party or date.

I only hung out with girlfriends and mostly concentrated on my classes until I graduated. The upside to that was I got great grades. If not for failing that one class, I would've graduated with honors."

They were quiet for a moment and Ginny stared down at her hand in Draper's. As his thumb moved over the side of her thumb, a warm glow bloomed inside of her. It was as if she had finally exorcised Trey Hartnet from the dark recesses of her being. She closed her eyes and tipped her face up to the soft morning breeze.

It was sometime later, when Ginny steered her car into the driveway and killed the engine, that she turned to Draper.

"For the record, my brothers don't know about this," she told him. "The only other person I've told is Kirby."

She resisted the urge to apologize for unloading on him. After what happened last night, he needed to know. Even more than that, she needed to talk about it with someone she cared about.

Draper nodded. "What we talk about is between you and me. Always."

He took her hands in his, lifted them to his lips and planted a soft, sweet kiss on her fingers.

As he got out of the car and headed back to his own house alone, Ginny knew that she was falling hard for Draper.

But what to do about it was another question.

* * *

Draper had only been inside his house for five minutes when someone rang the bell.

He smiled, thinking it might be Ginny. Maybe she'd forgotten to tell him something. He was grateful that she had confided in him. After what she'd shared with him, he hoped she felt free to come over without an invitation.

He'd only been away from her for a few minutes and he—he missed her. It might have just been the protective feelings she'd awakened in him. Protective, yes, but his feelings were anything but brotherly.

"May I help you?" he said, channeling the way Ginny had answered the door the Sunday morning after the gala.

But Ginny wasn't standing there. It was his brother Beau. Disappointment dropped like a cannonball in his gut.

"Look at you acting all formal and ringing the bell. Did Sofia teach you some manners?"

"I didn't want to barge in," Beau said. "Where the hell have you been all day?"

"Why the hell do you need to know?" Draper countered and stepped back so that Beau could follow him into the foyer.

"Because I've been trying to call you all morning," he said, shutting the door behind himself. "Why weren't you answering your phone? Your client, Tom English, wants in on the Nexus 500 Index Fund. He called me when he couldn't get ahold of you."

Draper frowned. "It's Sunday, for God's sake."

Beau knit his eyebrows together. "Since when do you take Sundays off?"

"When I want to have a day off. I am entitled to a day off every once in a while."

"Yeah, well, tell that to Tom English." Beau leaned toward Draper and sniffed the air. He made a face. "Something smells like horses. Why does it smell like a barn in here?"

"It doesn't smell like a barn in here." Draper imitated his brother's voice and pulled his cell out of his pocket. "I was out riding this morning. I turned off my phone and I forgot to turn it back on."

"Riding?" Beau screwed up his face. "You haven't been into horses since middle school, when you learned to ride to impress Jessica Hebert."

"I find the fact that you can remember the name of my seventh grade crush a little disturbing."

"Everyone had a crush on Jessica Hebert. You were just a little more proactive in going after what you wanted. So who's the horsey woman that got you back in the saddle?"

To punctuate the double entendre, Beau elbowed him.

Draper sat down on the couch. "I went riding with Ginny."

Beau's eyebrows raised like someone had pulled a cord. "Ginny next door?"

"Yes. Ginny Sanders."

Beau's gaze swept the room and landed on the

pair of to-go mugs that Draper had placed there after going riding with Ginny this morning. He intended to put them in the dishwasher after he showered.

"So she was your date to Macks's award shindig last night, and you two went riding early this morning. Did you spend the night together?"

"Not that it's any of your business, Sherlock Holmes," Draper said in his driest voice. "But she does live right next door."

"Right, which makes it awfully convenient to get cozy—"

"Hey, watch it." Draper didn't crack a smile. He wanted Beau to get the message loud and clear that he was serious about not kissing and telling when it came to Ginny. "I'm serious. Be careful there."

Not kissing and telling was the first of many things he intended to do to restore Ginny's faith and prove to her that not all men were monsters.

Chapter Ten

On Wednesdays, Rambling Rose High School dismissed an hour earlier than the other four days of the week. Draper had arranged to pick up Ginny to take her paintings to an art courier in Austin to ship them off to Macks for the show. After that, they were going for a late lunch at Provisions.

She'd worn a dress to school since there would be no time to change. It really must've been a noticeable change from her everyday look, because when she asked her second period American literature class if they had any questions, Farley Grant raised his hand and asked if she had a date after school.

She'd smiled and said, "I'm taking questions about *The Great Gatsby*. So unless you'd like extra homework, don't try to be cute."

When she looked down at her lesson plan to continue, she thought she heard someone murmur, "You look cute."

But she was in too good of a mood to get upset. So she pretended like she didn't hear the comment.

Actually, for the first time in a long time, she felt kind of cute, in her goldenrod-yellow dress that was flecked with tiny white flowers. She'd paired it with white flat sandals that showed off her toenails, which she'd recently painted with bright pink polish that she'd picked up at the drugstore. She'd twisted her long dark hair into a loose bun on top of her head and dug the gold hoop earrings her parents had given her for Christmas years ago out of her jewelry box. She loved them. Why had it been so long since she'd worn them?

They made her feel good.

In fact, the entire outfit made her feel good. It was pretty and feminine. Appropriate for school, and perfect for a lunch date. Because that's what this was.

A real date.

On Monday, Draper had called and asked her what she was doing after school on Wednesday. He hadn't just appeared at her door and expected her to be free. He'd called in advance. When she'd said she was shipping her work to Macks, he'd asked if he could join her and then take her for a late lunch because the occasion called for a celebration.

He looked so handsome in his khaki pants and black shirt. She was sort of surprised that he wasn't wearing his usual uniform of a dark suit, pressed white button-down and tie. But she was happy his casual, dressed-down look was on par with her slightly elevated style.

They'd met each other in the middle.

After sending off the paintings, they'd gone to Provisions. One of the town's first upscale restaurants, the place had opened a couple of years ago in a renovated grain warehouse. Even though Ginny had always wanted to try it, it was her first time there.

When they stepped inside and stopped at the hostess stand, Ginny glanced around, taking in the open and airy dining room with its high ceilings, exposed steel beams and rustic wooden interior. There were vintage photos on nearly every inch of wall space. She'd heard about them, how the sisters who had opened the place—another branch of the Fortune family—had worked hard to include photos of Rambling Rose residents, past and present, in the restaurant's design.

It was such a nice touch, a tribute to the town. As the hostess led them to a table, Ginny resisted the urge to lag behind and study the pictures. She could spend hours looking at them, trying to identify the subjects, but now wasn't the time. She didn't want to miss a minute with Draper.

Maybe she'd ask Kirby to meet her here for happy hour on their next girls' night out. Her friend would probably find the place just as intriguing as she did.

After Draper pulled out her chair and helped

her get settled, the hostess handed them menus and pointed out the large chalkboard hanging on the wall. It boasted the day's specials and a list of farm-to-table ingredients and the names of the local farmers from whom the restaurant had purchased the bounty.

"Your server will be right with you," the hostess said. "In the meantime, could I get your drinks?"

They both ordered iced tea and then began looking at the menu.

"This is so nice," Ginny said. "Thanks for suggesting it."

"My cousins Ashley, Megan and Nicole did a great job with the place," Draper said. "Owning a restaurant was their dream."

"Wow, that's fantastic," Ginny said. "But talk about taking a leap of faith."

As the server delivered their drinks and took their orders, a million questions—everything from how three women in their twenties managed to get financing for a place like this, to the actual logistics of setting up and opening a successful restaurant—pinged through her head, but each seemed more inappropriate and nosier than the next.

After the server left, she settled on a simple question. "I'm curious—how does someone with no experience open a business as risky as a restaurant and turn it into a thriving enterprise? It's a fact that most restaurants fail."

"My cousins didn't come into this completely green. They had worked in the business, each of them excelling in different aspects. Nicole is a chef. Ashley is a master at front of the house. Megan—" he nodded to the blond woman sitting at the bar eating a salad as she reviewed some papers "—is the business brains. She's the director of finance here and at Roja, over in the Hotel Fortune. But even with all of their experience combined, a restaurant consultant helped them get Provisions off the ground. And once that happened, Ashley married him."

He was referring to Ashley's marriage to Rodrigo Mendoza, which had almost been as big an event as the five weddings that had taken place on New Year's Eve.

They both laughed, but Ginny was thinking about how that event had been the impetus that had pushed her out of her comfort zone. If not for those five couples and being determined to step out of her own comfort zone, she might not be sitting here with Draper. The thought made her stomach somersault.

"Hey, I thought that was you," Beau Fortune said as he approached their table. "Hi, Ginny, it's good to see you."

"Good to see you, too, Beau."

"I'm sorry to interrupt," Beau said, "but have you spoken to Tom English today? He has some questions before he commits to the strategy we presented yesterday."

Since the restaurant was virtually empty at this hour and the brothers were talking shop, Ginny excused herself to take a closer look at one of the black and white photographs hanging on the wall near their table. In it, a dozen or so children, dressed in what looked like depression-era clothing, stood on the steps of an institutional-looking building. Two of the older children held babies. A blanket was draped over the legs of one of the infants.

Ginny gasped. Her eyes hadn't been playing tricks on her. That was definitely an *F* embroidered on the corner of the blanket. Since the photo wasn't in color, it was impossible to tell if the blanket was pink. Otherwise, it looked nearly identical to the one she'd seen on Draper's couch.

He had to see this.

She glanced over her shoulder at him. Beau was in the process of saying goodbye.

"See you later, Ginny," Beau called and was off after a quick wave.

"'Bye, Beau. Good to see you."

Ginny motioned for Draper to come over.

"What is it?" he asked and scooted his chair back.

"Look at this." She pointed to the photo. "Does anything look familiar?"

"Should I know those kids?" he asked as he joined her.

"Look at the blanket."

Draper leaned in. "Oh. It looks like that blanket someone sent to Beau." He looked back toward the door. "Man, I wish he could've seen this. I haven't even thought to ask him if he ever found out who sent the blanket."

He turned back to the photo again, pulled out his cell phone and snapped a picture of it. "I'll show it to him the next time I see him. I wonder who those kids are. Do you recognize them?"

"No," said Ginny. "I know all the people in these photos are local, but I don't recognize this group."

"Huh," Draper said. "I wonder if Megan knows anything about it. Let me go ask her. I'll be right back."

Ginny watched Draper confer with his cousin. From where she stood, she could hear him asking after Megan's new husband, Mark Mendoza.

"I have never been happier," Megan said.

Ginny could feel the joy in her voice. For a moment, she experienced a strange sense of longing, hoping that someday she would be so deliriously happy to be in love and to be loved that thoroughly by a man.

It was clear that Draper was happy for her. The fact that he was so dedicated to his family said a lot about him. Suddenly, a life with Draper flashed in her mind and it felt so right it almost brought her to tears.

As Megan asked Draper about his family, he told her that his sister Belle was engaged to Jack Radcliffe. When he added that she was no longer daydreaming about Mark's brother Stefan, it was a reality check that the Fortunes were a different breed. They had their choice of anyone they wanted.

It was a good reminder to Ginny not to "get above

her raisin'" as her grandmother used to say. It meant that she needed to not forget who she was and where she came from. She wanted to believe that this—this *thing* that was happening between Draper and her was something special. But she was smart enough to know she shouldn't read too much into his kindness. It was very possible that he was a truly nice guy who felt bad for her after she'd unloaded on him what had happened to her in college.

She needed to keep her heart in check so that she didn't end up on the same scrap heap as all of the other women he'd discarded.

A moment later Draper and Megan had returned to the table, and he introduced her to his cousin, who couldn't have been warmer and more gracious.

When Draper told her about the photo, Megan leaned in to get a closer look. Her face lit up. "Oh, yeah. That picture. I believe it was taken in front of the Fortune's Foundling Hospital. It was torn down in the eighties. The Rambling Rose Pediatric Center was built on its grounds."

Megan cocked her head to the side as she studied the picture.

"You know, let's ask Mariana about this. She's been in this town forever. If she doesn't know, I bet she could direct you to someone who does. She came over from Roja for a staff meeting. Let me run and see if she's still here. I'll be right back."

Ginny had known Mariana Sanchez her entire life. Mariana was beloved in Rambling Rose. While she didn't put up with nonsense, her larger-than-life personality endeared her to most people in town. It was a good bet that Mariana could give them some insight.

A few minutes later, Megan and Mariana emerged from the back. A full-figured middle-aged woman, Mariana had warm brown eyes and bleached blond hair that was pulled back into a bun.

"Which picture are you talking about?" Her voice carried through the restaurant.

"It's right over here." Megan led the way, but even before she had a chance to point out the photo, Mariana was nodding.

"I know which one you're talking about. The one with all the kids, right?"

"Yes, that's the one," said Megan as they approached. "Mariana, this is my cousin Draper Fortune. I don't know that you've officially met."

The two shook hands and exchanged pleasantries.

"And this is Ginny Sanders," Draper said.

Ginny waited for him to add a qualifier. "My friend," "my neighbor"—something to establish that they were...casual. That this was a lunch between friends. Nothing romantic.

But he didn't say it, and by that time, Mariana was going on about how she'd known Ginny and her family for years.

"You've got yourself a great gal there, Draper," Mariana said. "I hope you know how lucky you are."

Ginny's faced flamed as she held her breath waiting for Draper to deflect.

"Yes, ma'am," he said. "I know exactly how lucky I am."

Ginny could hear her heartbeat in her ears as it thudded against her chest and her toes curled in her sandals.

Then the conversation shifted to the photo.

"Yep, I'm pretty sure that's my mother, Maribel." Mariana pointed to the baby with the blanket. "I'm not one hundred percent sure, mind you, but I have a gut feeling."

Mariana leaned in and took another wistful look at the photo. "She's been gone for a long time now." She shrugged. "If it is her, I think Mama would be proud to have her photo right here among all the other fine citizens of her hometown."

Mariana waved her hand around in a gesture that seemed to indicate the whole town, rather than just the Provisions dining room.

Draper told her how a pink baby blanket had been delivered to his brother Beau last month.

"It looks a lot like the one in the photo," Draper said. "It has the same letter *F* monogram on it. What's odd is we have no idea who sent it or why."

Mariana blinked and looked puzzled.

"So, someone sent you a blanket like that?" she asked.

Draper nodded.

"Well, hold on to your hat," Mariana said. "Things are about to get even weirder."

The woman drew in a deep breath and exhaled before saying, "Someone sent me the same blanket, too. It was freaky since it was so similar to the one in the photo with the baby that I believe is my mother. But I didn't know who to talk to about it." She shook her head slowly. "So, Draper, your brother and I received these baby blankets. What do you think it means?"

Draper looked from Ginny to Megan to Mariana, as if they might know the answer. "I have no idea."

Mariana narrowed her eyes. "Okay, just go with me here. The first time I saw the photo, I couldn't figure out why my mother would've been at the Fortune foundling hospital. She never talked about it with me. But now, with all this baby blanket business..." Mariana hesitated. "Do you think... Well, what if I'm related to the Fortunes?"

Draper shrugged. "We need to find out who sent us the blankets. I mean, obviously this is all connected... somehow. Oh, my God, this is wild. Maybe we *are* related."

Mariana's cheeks flushed and her eyes were wide.

"Something to keep in mind is we're not the only members of the family who have received weird gifts," Draper said. "My cousin Brady got a horse sculpture from some anonymous sender. It ended up leading him to a safe-deposit box that contained a mysterious poem. My sister Belle got a framed print that said, 'A rose by any other name would smell as sweet.' Again, we have no clue who sent it. Now, we have to add the baby blankets that you and Beau received."

"Did you get anything?" Mariana asked him.

Draper shook his head. "No, thank God. We have enough pieces of this puzzle to put together without adding another one. If I organize a family meeting to try and figure this out, will you join us?"

Looking a little dazed, Mariana nodded.

"Good," Draper said. "We're going to get to the bottom of this one way or another."

Chapter Eleven

"May I see the blanket again?" Ginny asked after they pulled into his driveway and parked.

"Sure." This would be the first time they'd be alone in his house since she'd confided in him about what happened to her. Draper half expected her to suddenly remember and say "Oh! No, never mind."

When she didn't, he unlatched his seat belt and said, "Come on in."

As they walked to the door, he remembered, with almost painful clarity, that the last time they were alone in this house he'd kissed her, thinking he was giving part of himself to her. That they were opening a door that led to the next step. A step he didn't understand that he was actually taking.

He hated himself because as he held open the door for her, he wanted to kiss her again. He wouldn't, of course. Not unless she indicated that's what she wanted, too. The last thing he wanted was to make Ginny feel as if he was forcing himself on her.

She obviously trusted him. Why else would she ask to come in?

Oh, the blanket.

He led the way into the living room and tossed his keys on the coffee table.

"It's over there." He pointed to the exact spot where she'd folded it and placed it on the back of the sofa, and went into the kitchen.

"May I see the photo that you snapped with your phone?"

"Sure." He took the phone out of his pocket and held it out it to her. Wearing a strange half smile, Ginny looked at the phone and then at him.

"Don't you want to look at it?" she asked.

He did, but he didn't want to crowd her. Of course, if she felt crowded or compromised, would she even be here alone with him?

"Um, yeah," he said. "Sure."

"Are you okay?" she asked. "I didn't even ask you if this was a good time for me to come in. Maybe I'm keeping you from something?"

She refolded the blanket and returned it to its spot on the sofa. "I just realized maybe you need to take care of whatever it was that you and Beau were talking about at the restaurant. Sorry, I should've thought of that. I'll leave you to what you need to do." She picked up her purse from the chair where she'd set it and started toward the door. "Thank you for lunch—"

"No. You're not keeping me from anything, Ginny. Please don't go. Unless you want to. But I'd really like for you to stay."

She stopped, but her back was still toward him. "Are you sure?"

"Yes, I'm sure."

She turned to face him.

"Draper, since we got in here, I've sensed something. I mean, we had such a nice time at lunch. And I know there's the weird coincidence with the photo of the blanket and Mariana, but—"

"I want you to be here," he said. "But..."

"But what? Is this about what I told you? Did I say too much? Should I not have told you what happened to me?"

She bit her bottom lip as if she regretted asking the question. Then, once again, she was moving toward the door.

"Ginny, wait. Please."

Her hand was on the knob, but she stopped.

"Actually, I'm glad you asked me that. No, absolutely not. I am so happy you felt comfortable enough to confide in me. But I have to be honest with you. I don't quite know what to do. The last time we were here together, I kissed you and you ran. I understand why, but I need to know what to do. How to move forward. The last thing I'd ever want to do is make you feel uncomfortable, but the truth is I want to kiss you again. I just don't want to—"

She turned around and walked back. She let her purse fall to the floor, then put both hands on his cheeks and kissed him so thoroughly that the entire world seemed to tilt on its axis and spin faster and faster, until all he could do was hold on to her for dear life. He pulled her closer and lost himself in the feel of her lips on his, his hands on her body, her body so close to his that he didn't know where one of them stopped and the other started.

Until the faint ringing of a bell pulled him back to earth.

It took a moment, but when the bell sounded again, he realized that someone was at the door.

"No one is home," he murmured over her lips.

When it sounded a third time, Ginny stepped back. Looking a little dazed, she said, "You'd better get that."

He must've looked unconvinced because she said, "This time I promise I won't run."

He leaned in and dusted a quick kiss over her lips. "I'm going to hold you to that. Stay right here."

When he answered the door, a deliveryman was walking back to his truck with a package. "Hey! I'm home," Draper called. "Sorry to keep you waiting."

"No problem," the guy said. "Normally, I'd just leave the package, but this one asks for a signature. You Draper Fortune?"

"I am." Draper racked his brain, trying to remember if he'd ordered something. He couldn't recall anything. Usually, he and Beau had packages delivered to the office. Strange. Maybe his mother had sent him something. It would be just like her to send a care package. But this one was flat—about the size of a pizza box.

After Draper signed for it, he looked for a return address on the package, but there wasn't one.

"Excuse me," he called to the delivery guy. "There's no return address. Is there any way I can find out who sent this?"

"Sorry, man, I don't have any records like that. There might be a note inside?"

"Good thought. Thanks."

"I got a package," Draper said after he brought it into the house. "Let's open it and see what it is."

With a pair of scissors, he cut the tape on the box. Inside a protective layer of bubble wrap was a record album. "Okay, this is odd on so many levels," he said. "I definitely didn't order it. I don't even own a record player."

Draper moved some extra bubble wrap out of the box and found a business card with the name of the company that shipped it, a store in Austin that dealt in vinyl. He called the phone number on the card.

"I just received a package from your store. It looks like a record album of some sort. The sleeve doesn't say what the album is and there wasn't any indication of the sender in the box. I wanted to make sure it was actually for me before I opened the plastic seal. Can you tell me who sent it?"

He gave his name and address, and a moment later, the guy came back on the line.

"Sorry, dude. The records say the person paid cash and asked it to be delivered to Draper Fortune. That's you, right?"

"That's me."

"I wasn't the one who sold it. So I don't know what to tell you except enjoy."

Draper disconnected the call and relayed the details to Ginny.

"The guy has a point," she said. "You might as well enjoy it. I wonder if the Dobsons have a record player?"

They both glanced around the living room.

"I don't remember seeing one in the house," Draper said. "But there's a bunch of stuff out in the garage. Let's go have a look."

The Dobsons' garage was full of boxes from wall to wall.

"They rented us the house fully furnished," Draper said. "But these are their personal things that they packed away. I don't want to open any of the boxes. Let's just look on the shelves."

They didn't find a record player, but Ginny pointed to an old boom box on a shelf near the door.

"You know what that reminds me of?" she asked.

"That eighties movie, *Say Anything*?"

She nodded.

"My brother and I were talking about that movie recently," Draper said. "I haven't seen it in ages."

"It's so good. Personally, I think it's the most romantic of all the eighties movies."

"I didn't know there was a single eighties movie that was romantic," Draper said.

"Hey, don't judge. It's my favorite."

He smiled. "It is?"

She nodded.

"Well, if you're not doing anything tomorrow night, how about if I make dinner for us and we can watch it?"

Ginny smiled. "I think that sounds great. And I just happen to have a copy of the DVD. That soundtrack has Peter Gabriel's 'In Your Eyes.' I love that song."

"Yeah, that's a good one," he said. "Maybe dinner and a movie will prove to you that I don't only attend black-tie events in my spare time."

"Speaking of songs, what album did you get in that package?"

"I don't know," he said. "The sleeve isn't marked and the plastic is sealed. Let's open it and see."

They went back into the house, and as Draper carefully used the tip of the scissors to open the plastic, Ginny said, "Do you think this has anything to do with all the other weird presents your family has been receiving?"

"I don't know. It is odd, though."

When he pulled the record from the sleeve, it, too, was unmarked.

"There's no label on the record." Holding the vinyl by the edges, Draper turned it over to see if there was something on the other side. It was also blank. "All the other items that my family received seemed like they were related in some way. Some were marked with an *F* like the blanket that Beau got or the picture of the rose that was sent to Belle had *MAF* inscribed on it. Until we can find a record player and figure out what's on this album, there's really nothing to connect it to the other items besides the fact that it's a random gift from an anonymous giver."

Even so, Draper's gut told him there had to be a connection.

The next night, Draper did an admirable job of fixing chicken piccata. She couldn't imagine a guy who was used to eating in the finest restaurants rolling up his sleeves and getting his hands dirty. If not for the mess in the kitchen—because it looked as though he'd used every pot, pan and utensil in the place—she might have thought that he'd ordered in from Osteria Oliva, the Italian restaurant in The Shoppes, a shopping center in Rambling Rose. But no one could fake a mess like that.

With Draper, one thing was constant. He continued to be full of surprises.

"That was delicious," Ginny said. "If you ever wanted to get into the restaurant business, you could give Carla Vicente a run for her chicken piccata."

When his brow creased, she explained that Carla was the owner of Osteria Oliva.

"No, I'll leave that to my cousins," Draper said. "I've seen how hard they work at Provisions and Roja. It's a good thing they all found spouses, otherwise they'd be married to their jobs."

"Where did you learn to cook like that?" Ginny asked as they took their wine and moved from the table over to the sofa.

He sipped his wine and leaned forward, resting his forearms on his legs. "I took a cooking class a few years ago when I was in Florence on business. Full disclosure, other than a particularly killer loaded baked potato that I make in the microwave and the chicken piccata I prepared for you, I don't really cook. I mostly grab dinner and lunch while I'm out. But changing the subject for just a moment, what are you doing this weekend?"

She blinked at the sudden shift in conversation. "This weekend, as in Saturday or Sunday?"

"This weekend as in between after school tomorrow to Sunday evening."

Ginny's mind raced. Was he going to suggest they go away for the weekend? Warmth spread from her chest to her neck in a prickly rush. "The usual, I guess. Why?"

"How would you feel about going somewhere?"

She laughed. "Where?"

He arched an eyebrow. "It's a surprise."

Now that she knew that's exactly what he had in

mind, a million emotions flooded through her. A whole weekend with Draper…just the two of them. Her heart hammered and pounded and bounced around her chest so hard that she was afraid he would be able to feel the vibrations, since he was sitting so close.

Would going away with him mean he would expect them to take their relationship to the next level? As in sleeping with him? Was she ready for that? There hadn't been anyone since—since that night she refused to let dictate her life.

That meant she wouldn't let a monster like Trey Hartnet stand in the way of something with a good man like Draper Fortune.

But was she really ready?

Women threw themselves at Draper. He could probably walk out that door right now and find a handful of women in Rambling Rose who would be thrilled to go away with him for the weekend…and give him all that entailed.

"If you're worried about sleeping accommodations," he said, as if reading her mind, "you don't have to be. I'm not going to force you into anything you're not ready for. But I do have a fantastic surprise in mind."

Oh, there was that smile. It ignited a traitorous zing that ricocheted through her veins and created a warmth, the likes of which she hadn't felt in ages. It pooled in her most private, personal parts and urged her to consider the possibility.

Maybe she was ready to try again.

Maybe.

He has a surprise. For me.

"I do love surprises," she said.

At the thought of opening herself to the possibility of Draper, it felt like her hammering heart broke free, leaped out of her body and swung from the midcentury modern chandelier in the Dobson living room.

She had been living so safely in her cocoon for so long that she couldn't remember the last time she'd allowed anything to surprise her.

"Is that a yes?" he asked, looking up at her through those thick, dark lashes.

She nodded.

"Great, can you be ready to go after school tomorrow?"

"What should I pack?" she asked.

"Keep it fairly casual, but maybe a couple of nicer dresses."

She raised her eyebrows. "Nicer as in black-tie?"

She was already trying to figure out how she could call Anna and ask her if she could borrow that dress again, when Draper laughed.

"Not black-tie. Nicer as in something you'd wear out on a weekend."

She scratched Anna off her mental to-do list and added Kirby. It would be much more manageable to borrow the little black dress she'd worn to the Austin Arts Gala. She could drop by the coffeehouse tomorrow morning before school.

Draper pushed Play on the DVD player remote, then settled back on the couch and put one arm around Ginny.

This was an honest-to-goodness date, which would be followed by a weekend away. As they watched the movie, she kept thinking about that and waiting for him to lean in and kiss her. Every so often she would glance at him, hoping to send the signal that it was fine with her if he did just that… It would be preferable, actually.

He was so good to her. So patient and gentle. Her heart was so full.

She was falling for him.

Falling hard.

And that was okay… No, it was more than okay, it felt right.

She studied his profile, thinking about how much she wanted him to touch her, but he seemed lost in the movie. Though she couldn't tell if he liked it or not. When it was over, she reached up and ran a finger over his creased forehead.

"You hated the movie," she said.

"I didn't *hate* it."

"Then why are you making that face?"

"I'm not making a face," he said.

"Oh, really? Usually when someone scowls like this—" she scrunched up her face in an exaggerated version of Draper's frown "—it's usually a good indication they're not really into whatever it is they're glowering at. Did you hate it?"

He laughed. "I wouldn't go so far as to say I *hated* it," he said. "That's a strong word. Lloyd and Diane were kind of mismatched."

"It was a classic case of opposites attract."

Kind of like us.

She couldn't bring herself to say that because it sounded like she thought they were a couple.

Instead, she said, "You can't deny that the boom box scene outside of Diane's window was romantic."

"You don't think it was a pathetic display of weakness?" he said.

"Absolutely not." Ginny swatted his leg. "Lloyd was in love with Diane and he would do anything to win her back."

"Maybe he should've gotten a job instead of relying on a boom box."

"Maybe he did end up getting a job," Ginny said.

"Maybe he did." Draper reached out and touched Ginny's face. She could feel the heat of his fingers all the way to her core.

"You've got to admit 'In Your Eyes' is one of the best love songs of all time," she whispered.

"Yes, it is."

She angled toward him, hoping he understood what she really wanted. As if answering her, he turned to meet her. The kiss started slow and soft. The whisper of a kiss, really. Tender and slow, with brushes of lips and hints of tongue that made her heart pound and her body say *Yes*!

Draper tasted like heaven, and she ignored the

vague buzz in her head warning her that she knew what kissing a man could lead to. And that's when she knew what she wanted. More. She didn't want Draper to stop.

As if he read her mind, the gentle brushes of his lips grew more urgent, and she parted her lips to deepen the kiss. She fisted her hands into his shirt, pulling their bodies even closer, clinging to him as if her next life breath would come from him and him alone. He held her so tight that for a moment, she melted into the heat of him, the smell of him. The combination threatened to drive her over the edge.

Feelings she thought had died were bustling and blossoming into a passion that eclipsed her once logical rationale for protecting her heart. All those reasons *why not* began to splinter and fall away, until there was nothing left except raw need and desire.

Ginny had no idea how much time had passed when they finally came up for air.

She didn't know if it was because of the wine, the banter or the kiss—or the synergy of the three—but she loved the way he made her feel…the rush she felt when he touched her. She hadn't felt this alive since…

Well, it had been way too long.

She was finally sure that she wanted all of Draper Fortune. She wanted him to have all of her.

That's why it threw her when he pulled away, breathless and gasping, raking his hand over his face as if he were trying to get ahold of himself.

"What's wrong?" she asked.

He scooted away, putting some distance between them. "I think we'd better call it a night," he said.

When she didn't say anything, he said, "Ginny, I want you. I mean, I really want you, but I don't want to rush you. But kissing you like this—"

He squeezed his eyes shut. When he opened them, he stood up suddenly and shook his head.

So did she. "Draper, I want you to make love to me."

"Are you sure?" Draper asked. "It won't change anything between us if you leave. I want you to be ready."

Ginny pressed her finger to his lips. The look in her eyes told him all he needed to know.

The need to touch her was driving him insane.

"Are you sure?" he asked one more time.

"Shhh... Yes."

She put her hands on his chest and then swept her fingers over his shoulders and down his arms, leaving a trail of goose flesh in their wake. When her hands moved to his butt, and she pulled him in so close that his hardness was pressing into her, a low moan escaped his throat.

She answered him with a kiss that was so sweet it almost broke his heart.

He lifted her up in one swift scoop of legs and derriere, and carried her to his bedroom, where he eased her onto the bed. It was madness how much he wanted her.

Sheer, unadulterated madness.

His lips explored her neck for a few glorious moments before his mouth reclaimed her lips again, capturing her tongue, teasing her until he thought he might come undone.

He made quick work of getting rid of her blouse and bra, which was light blue and lacy and totally sexy. His shirt fell away, too.

Nothing compared to the feel of her bare skin next to his, except maybe how perfectly they seemed to fit together. He smoothed a lock of hair off her forehead, kissed the skin he uncovered, then searched her eyes. "Are you sure, Ginny?" he asked one final time.

"I've never been more certain of anything in my entire life," Ginny said.

It had been a long time since she'd wanted a man this way. She wanted his kiss… His touch… His body… All of him.

He lifted her chin and kissed her softly, gently, until she was overcome with a need so consuming it eclipsed everything else.

Just him and her.

Her lips on his.

His hands on her body.

She relished the glide of his touch sweeping down

her body then inching underneath her to claim her bottom and pull her closer.

For the first time in ages she felt…safe.

And turned on.

Yes, definitely turned on.

No thoughts of the past… No thoughts of the future.

Just now.

Right here, right now with Draper and this need that was driving her wild.

He kissed her neck and that tender spot behind her ear before claiming her mouth again, capturing her bottom lip between his teeth, teasing her tongue with his until the rest of her body begged for his attention.

Her fingers swept over his shoulders and muscled arms before exploring the dip of his back and the rise of his butt. It didn't seem possible, but he managed to pull her even closer so that the hardness of him pressed into her, urging her legs to part and invite him in.

She needed him now, but he moved onto his side and kissed her breasts. His fingers moved from one nipple to the other, finally trailing down her belly, where they lingered and played, tracing small circles that made her stomach muscles tighten and spasm in agonizing pleasure.

Then his hand dipped farther still, teasing its way down, edging toward the hidden place that begged for his touch.

Gently, his fingers slid inside her, searching, stroking, coaxing one moan after another from her until her entire body shuddered and liquefied like wax at the flame of his touch.

"Are you okay?" he asked.

She nodded because she couldn't quite form the words that described how she felt right now.

She'd never been better.

She ached for more.

So much more.

As if he'd heard her unspoken plea, he took a condom from his nightstand drawer and rolled it on. He covered her body with his, nestling himself between her legs. She marveled at how perfectly they fit together.

From his first gentle thrust until the moment they went over the edge together, he was the perfect combination of tender and voracious.

Once she'd been certain she'd never be able to feel this way again, but she did.

The reality brought tears to her eyes.

As they lay there, satisfied and spent, Draper held her so close that she swore she could hear his heartbeat.

Or maybe it was her heart beating in time with his. All she knew was she felt safe and warm and… undamaged. It was as if he had gathered up all of her broken pieces and put her back together.

For the first time in a very long time, she felt whole again.

* * *

Draper saw the tears glistening in Ginny's blue eyes.

"Are you okay?" he asked.

She smiled, looking more beautiful than he'd ever seen her.

"I've never been better."

Her words were a breathless whisper. Coupled with the tears, her reaction simultaneously touched and scared him.

Sex with Ginny was more intimate than what he was used to. It was wonderful, but terrifying.

As he put his arms around her and pulled her closer, she nuzzled into him.

Why did something so beautiful have to be so complicated? How could it be both wonderful and terrifying?

As Ginny snuggled closer, Draper stared into the murky distance, trying to shake off the familiar claustrophobia that threatened to suffocate him.

He would never purposely hurt her. After all she'd been through, only a monster would do that.

Even as he planted a tender kiss on the top of her head, he couldn't silence the monster inside him that was roaring, *Oh, God, Fortune, what have you done?*

Chapter Twelve

Ginny felt like a teenager sneaking in when she got home from Draper's house at four thirty in the morning.

It was difficult to drag herself out of the warmth of Draper's strong arms, but she knew if it got any later, she would risk the neighbors seeing her leaving his house at that hour and that would set off a quake of gossip that would probably make its way around the world to Japan, where her parents were teaching.

She was twenty-seven years old and certainly not a child, but things were so new with Draper, she wanted their relationship to stay private at least until it had a chance to take root.

Maybe that would happen this weekend.

She had never been happier that her brother Jerry slept like the dead, because it would be hard to explain why she was up so early and why she couldn't stop smiling like an idiot.

After she showered and got ready for school, Ginny worked as quickly as she could, knocking out the day's painting and packing for their weekend away. She even packed a small art travel kit with three colors of paint and one brush so she could stay on track while she was away. She wanted to have everything ready so all they had to do was grab their bags and go after school let out.

She texted Kirby and asked if she could borrow the dress again. Since her friend had to get the girls ready for school and then open the coffee shop, she knew she would be up before the sun.

"Where is he taking you?" Kirby's eyes sparkled as she handed Ginny the black dress later at the coffeehouse. It was still in the dry cleaner's plastic from when Ginny had given it back to her.

"I don't know," said Ginny. "It's a surprise." Again, the smile that had commandeered her lips since she had left Draper's house this morning took over.

Kirby smiled back. "It's wonderful to see you so happy. Honestly, I can't remember the last time I saw you like this."

She hesitated and cleared her throat.

"What?" Ginny asked.

Kirby looked at her for a moment, as if carefully

considering her words before she spoke. "You know I love you, and that's the only reason I'm asking you this, but are you sure you're ready to take this step? Are you ready to go away with him for an entire weekend?"

Ginny couldn't suppress her joy. "Kirby, I'm so ready for this."

Around eight o'clock Friday morning, someone knocked on Draper's front door.

He was in the middle of cleaning up the dinner dishes from the night before. If there was anything he enjoyed less than cooking, it was cleaning up the mess afterward.

As he dried his hands, he reminded himself there was no use grousing over it now. He just needed to get in there and get it done. His housekeeper wouldn't come until the middle of next week, and he was leaving for New Orleans this afternoon. There was a lot to do to get ready, including making sure he didn't leave the mess over the weekend.

Before he could reach the door, his brother Beau let himself in and called, "Good morning."

For some inexplicable reason, that irritated Draper.

What if Ginny had still been here?

He frowned and said in a flat voice, "Come right in. Make yourself at home."

Beau flinched, but before he could answer, Draper turned and walked back into the kitchen.

He heard his brother follow him.

"Sorry, I didn't realize I needed to wait for you to let me in. I used to live here, you know."

"Yeah, well, I don't just barge into your house without knocking."

"I knocked," Beau said. "And I live with Sofia in her condo. That's a completely different situation than this."

"What if I'd had a woman here? That does happen occasionally."

"Clearly." Beau gestured around the kitchen and eyed the mess. "Did you have company last night?"

"Maybe." Draper scraped the remnants of last night's chicken piccata into the sink and used a spatula to poke it down the garbage disposal.

"Given your mood," Beau said, "it must not have gone well."

"Who says it didn't go well? And I'm not in a mood. I'm just stressed. I have to clean up this mess. I need to pack, and I have several things I have to take care of at the office before I leave for New Orleans this afternoon."

"Okay, so you are leaving today? That's what I came by to ask."

"You could've called. You didn't have to come all the way over here."

"You've been a little hard to reach the last few days. I've called you a couple of times since I saw you at the restaurant with Ginny, but you haven't called me back."

"Yes. We're leaving today. I chartered a plane because the artists' reception is tonight. It's important that Ginny is there. This is a big deal for her."

Beau's brows lifted.

"Was Ginny the one who was here last night?"

Draper turned to face his brother.

"That's none of your business."

"I mean, I know you allow yourself a certain amount of freedom in your dating life, but I can't imagine that you'd sandwich a sleepover with another woman in between a lunch date and a weekend out of town with Ginny."

An inexplicable feeling of protectiveness reared up like a bear inside him. He wasn't about to kiss and tell and violate Ginny's privacy. Not even to his own brother.

"Besides, I talked to Mom this morning and she said the two of you are staying at the house. So it must be serious if you're taking her home to meet the parents?" Beau said.

"I think you'd better go," Draper answered. "I have a lot to do and I'm sure you do, too."

Not to mention he was fighting the overwhelming urge to stuff the dirty dishcloth in his brother's mouth to stop him from saying anything else.

"Come on, Draper, this is great news. Ginny is fantastic. And look at you all tight-lipped and gentlemanly. I've never seen you like this over a woman."

Draper turned away and cranked the knob on the

sink so that the water flowed full blast and muffled Beau's words.

But his brother talked louder. "That's what being in love will do to you."

"You are so barking up the wrong tree. I am not in love. Not even a little bit." Even saying the words made him panic like he was caught in a windowless room that was on fire. "I'm sure Ginny will be great for someone, but not for me. So, let's just nip this discussion in the bud right now. Got it? And unless you'd like to help me finish cleaning the kitchen, you'd better go."

"Okay. Got it, bro." Beau looked like he was going to say something else, but Draper turned away. A moment later, he heard the sound of the front door opening and closing.

Draper mentally kicked himself. He was such an idiot.

When he'd told his mom he'd be home for the weekend, she'd insisted that he and his "friend" stay there. She had plenty of room and that way, at least, she'd get to see him between the events at the gallery.

It was no wonder that Beau would read something more into it than what it was.

The monster inside him that had stirred last night and said, *What the hell are you doing?*, the one he'd tried to push down, was roaring now and telling him that after what happened last night, Ginny might get the wrong idea about meeting his parents, too.

* * *

Draper had chartered a plane to take them to New Orleans for the weekend so that Ginny could attend the opening of the show at Macks's gallery.

They'd boarded the private jet at Austin Executive Airport and less than an hour and a half later they'd touched down at Lakefront Airport in New Orleans, which, Draper pointed out, was just five miles northeast of downtown New Orleans.

She couldn't even drive to Waco, Texas, in an hour and a half.

She pushed down a little voice inside of her that said, *I could get used to this.* She didn't want to get used to it because she didn't want to be like the other women Draper had dated that seemed so captivated by all the things money could buy.

Since that thought was a major buzz kill, she decided not to think of the women in Draper's past. Especially since they were not staying in a hotel this weekend, but in his family home in the Garden District.

Meeting his parents was a huge step in their relationship, Ginny thought. She wished she'd known they were going straight to the Fortune house, because she would've freshened up before getting into the car that was waiting at the airport to whisk them away.

She took a deep breath and reminded herself that Draper seemed to like her because she was different from all the women in his past.

On the way from the airport, Draper said, "Even though my parents are empty nesters, they still live in the house where my brothers and sisters and I grew up. Even though it's way too much house for just two people, my mother won't hear of moving. As far as she's concerned, it's our family home and she doesn't want to live anywhere else."

And, boy, *was* it a lot of house. Neither Ginny's imagination nor Draper's explanation had prepared her for the majesty of the rambling Victorian Garden District mansion that appeared before them.

As the driver steered the car through the stately iron gates that surrounded the home and grounds, butterflies swooped and swarmed in her stomach.

"Welcome to our humble abode," said Draper.

"You're being ironic, right?"

He answered her with a laugh.

After the baggage was on the porch, Draper pushed open the front door, which looked like it was made of Tiffany glass, and they stepped into a stunning foyer. Straight ahead was an antique wooden console with a vase of the most gorgeous fresh flowers Ginny had ever seen. It looked like it should've been on a table at the Ritz. She wished she could paint them, right then and there.

"Hello," he called.

Ginny heard the sound of heels tapping on wood and soon a petite redheaded woman appeared. She was wearing a crisp green linen blouse over a pair of slim black leggings. Her hair was pulled back away from her pretty face, and diamond studs on her ears and a rock on her left hand sparkled as she clapped in delight.

"You're finally here." She opened her arms. "Come here and give your mama a hug. Oh, it's so good to see you."

After she stepped back, she turned her congenial smile on Ginny.

"This must be your artist friend, Ginny. I'm Draper's mother, Sarah Fortune." She took Ginny's hands in both of hers and gave them a squeeze, as the words *your artist friend* rang in Ginny's ears.

What was he supposed to tell his mother about their relationship? "Hey, Mom, this is my lover...?" But would it have been so bad if he'd introduced her as his girlfriend?

At least his mother knew her name.

"Hello, Mrs. Fortune. It's nice to meet you. Thank you for letting me stay in your beautiful home."

"Of course, it's so nice to have you." Sarah motioned to the suitcases. "Draper, be a dear and take the bags upstairs. I'll show Ginny to Belle's room."

Oh.

Ginny was surprised by the ridiculous twist of disappointment she felt at having her own room. Had she really been expecting his mother to put them in the same room? Of course not. It was probably just the expectation of going away for the weekend with Draper. But, truthfully, this was actually very sweet.

It might even be a little exciting to have him sneak into her bed at night.

A modest arrangement of fresh flowers, a small box of chocolates, a bottle of water and a crystal glass were laid out on a tray on the bedside table. Sarah showed her to the ensuite bathroom and pointed out the towels and toiletries that Ginny was welcome to use.

"Since it's just Draper's father and me, I don't employ a staff," she said. "So if you need anything, don't hesitate to ask me. I want you to be comfortable."

With that, she left the two of them with apologies. "My husband is out of town and I have an engagement tonight, but I look forward to seeing both of you tomorrow. Your father will be home. Maybe we could have dinner?"

"I don't know, Mom," Draper said. "This weekend is all about Ginny's art. Can we play it by ear?"

All about my art?

Surely they had time for dinner with his folks. She was about to insist, but a look that passed between him and his mom stopped her. Maybe she'd misinterpreted it.

After they were alone, Draper said, "The artists' reception starts at seven. There'll probably be some press there, too. I thought we'd go to the gallery and then go for a late dinner afterward. Why don't you get changed and I'll meet you downstairs in an hour."

"Sounds like a plan. Draper, tomorrow I'd love

to have dinner with your parents. It was so sweet of your mom to invite us. I'd love to meet your dad."

He shrugged. "We'll see."

With that, she had a sinking feeling she hadn't misinterpreted his look at all.

They arrived at Macks's gallery, Chanson de Vache, shortly after seven. It was a contemporary spot set in an ancient-looking, three-story building located in New Orleans's warehouse arts district. The gallery's shop front was made up of sidewalk-to-ceiling glass panels that gave the place an open, airy appearance.

The invitation said seven, but the gallery was already crowded with people spilling into the street with wineglasses in their hands or bellied up to small round cocktail tables set up on the sidewalks, next to the whitewashed brick building, so as not to block the view of the party through the windows.

Were all these people potential art buyers?

Not all of them, surely. The majority looked like they were twentysomethings, which seemed young to have disposable income for art, but they were well dressed in artsy hip fashion.

Ginny shrank into herself, feeling as if she'd missed the style mark again. The last time she'd worn Kirby's gorgeous dress, she'd felt underdressed among all the women in ballgowns. But that night her understated LBD had worked, despite its minimalist design. Tonight, she felt as if she was on her way to a homecoming dance, but had ended up at fashion week.

The woman directly to Ginny's left was wearing a modified version of the infamous *Seinfeld* "puffy shirt." Only the tiered ascot had been removed and the bodice had been trimmed and cinched into a midriff-baring crop top. But the sleeves were one hundred percent *Seinfeld.* She'd paired it with silky black harem-style pants and stilettos so high that Ginny half expected her to topple over.

Another woman was wearing a pair of high-waisted gunmetal-gray pants with a top that looked like chain mail—very loose chain mail that left little to the imagination. Yet another woman wore a form-fitting black turtleneck dress with holes cut into the neck, bodice and sleeves. The cutouts made Ginny think of Swiss cheese, which perfectly summed up Ginny's fashion aptitude.

All this and she hadn't even entered the gallery.

Once inside, the fashion parade continued, but it was so crowded and so difficult to move around that Ginny realized people really couldn't see what she was wearing. Besides, in situations like this, weren't some people too consumed with what people thought of them to notice how others were dressed?

Ginny smiled at the idea as she glanced around and looked for Macks, who was nowhere in sight. Draper seemed to know everyone in the place. Ginny wasn't surprised. That's how it was for her in Rambling Rose. She couldn't go anywhere without seeing someone she knew. It was interesting to see Draper in his element, and a little strange, because even though he'd only lived in Texas a few months, Ginny had begun to think of him as a Rambling Rose resident.

"Hey, Leo, it's good to see you again," Draper said to a guy who looked to be about his own age. They shook hands and drew each other into a loose bro hug.

"Where have you been, Fortune?" the guy asked. "It's been ages."

"Actually, I'm living in Texas now. I'm home for the weekend. I want to introduce you to my friend Ginny Sanders. She's an artist. A few of her paintings are in the show tonight."

She and Leo exchanged pleasantries.

"Which paintings are yours?" he asked.

"I have a trio of floral abstracts," she said. "I'm not sure where they are. We just arrived and we haven't made our way around to see the art yet."

Leo's gaze darted around the room as Ginny talked. He didn't really seem interested in what she had to say. Ginny got the feeling he'd asked because it was the polite thing to do in a social situation like this. Similar to someone asking "How are you?" but not really caring to hear the answer.

But she gave Leo the benefit of the doubt, since there was a lot going on in the crowded space. So many people were talking and laughing, and it was hard to hear.

As a server passed by with a tray of champagne flutes, Draper grabbed two glasses and handed one to Ginny. Leo also grabbed two.

"Are you here with someone?" Ginny asked Leo.

"No. I just want to make sure they don't run out before they pass by here again."

Ginny smiled, unsure what to say to that, but it didn't matter. Draper and Leo seemed to have a lot to catch up on. They spoke in low tones, and because of the din, she only caught a word or three here and a snippet of conversation there. But there was no missing the willowy platinum blonde who walked up behind Draper and put her hands over his eyes. She had no problem hearing when the blonde said, "Guess who, lover?"

Draper turned around and exclaimed, "Astrid! Oh, my God!"

He pulled her into a hug and she planted a kiss on his lips. It wasn't exactly a chaste kiss, either, and afterward Astrid proceeded to hang on him.

Something green and thorny sprouted in Ginny's solar plexus.

"Draper Fortune, where have you been?" Astrid scolded. She had one of those voices that transcended mere mortals. "I thought you'd ghosted me."

"I didn't ghost you. I moved to Texas. Beau and I opened a branch of Fortune Investments outside of Austin."

"Oh, Austin," she said. "How fun. What's it like

to live there? Are you doing your part to keep Austin weird?"

They laughed.

Ginny wanted to roll her eyes.

The cliché hit her about the same way it would if Ginny had exclaimed, *"Laissez les bon temps rouler"* to Astrid.

"I don't live in Austin per se," Draper said. "I'm in a place called Rambling Rose."

Astrid scrunched up her pert little nose. "Where the hell is Rambling Rose? Sounds like the middle of nowhere."

Draper chuckled. "It's a small town, true, but it's got charms of its own. Plus, it's halfway between Austin and Houston, so the location is convenient to our clients if nothing else. But if my cousins hadn't opened a restaurant god knows where I'd find anything to eat."

Wow. Okay, Mr. Big Stuff.

Who was this snob and what had he done with Draper?

"I'm renting a house," he continued. "I'll reevaluate when the lease is up. Who knows, Miles might summon me home."

A disappointed ache pressed up from Ginny's stomach to her heart. That was the first she'd heard of his stay possibly being temporary.

"Good. Move back home." Astrid cupped his face with her hands and Ginny feared she was going to kiss him again. "I've missed your gorgeous face too much."

Astrid suddenly dropped her hands. "Oh, but have you talked to Simone? You know she's pissed off at you. I tried to get her to come tonight, but she had other plans. She's going to be so mad when she finds out that I saw you and she missed a chance to throw a drink in your face."

Draper frowned.

Astrid smiled coyly and ducked her head, looking up at him through her lashes. "Look, I know the two of you were in a bad place the last time you saw each other, but you know what? I don't blame her for being mad."

Who the heck is Simone and what did Draper do to her?

When Ginny glanced at Draper, she realized that somewhere between Astrid's kiss hello and the mention of Simone, his demeanor had hardened…and Ginny had become invisible.

"So, anyway, we're having a party tomorrow," Astrid said. "Show up and surprise her. It's the least you can do."

"I can't. I am here with a friend for the weekend. Oh, man, I'm sorry. Ginny, I didn't even introduce you."

Yeah, hello?

"Astrid, this is my friend Ginny Sanders."

There was the *F* word again.

His friend.

Awesome.

The same way he'd introduced her to his mom and Leo. Only this time it was hard to not take it personally. Because was it really so out of line to think of herself as his girlfriend after they'd made love and he'd whisked her away for this surprise weekend, which, as things were unfolding, seemed to be less about the two of them and more about him reconnecting with his NOLA friends.

Why had he brought her home to meet his mom? She'd obviously read more into that than she should have. After all, he'd introduced her as "my friend Ginny."

But what was she supposed to think? Draper Fortune certainly was the king of mixed messages.

Even though she ached inside, Ginny smiled.

"Ginny, this is my good friend, Astrid. She and I go way back."

Oh! So Astrid was his *good* friend. There was a hierarchy. Nice.

She gave Ginny's dress a judgmental once-over and forced a smile. Clearly, Astrid did not play well with other women. Except for Simone, obviously, but her motives there seemed questionable, too.

"We do go way back, don't we?" Astrid tipped up her chin and batted her lashes at Draper. Seriously, she batted. "Way, way, way back."

She laughed and it took every ounce of Ginny's self-control not to *accidentally* spill champagne down the front of the woman's expensive-looking pink-and-white polka-dot boho peasant blouse, which she'd paired with shorts and heels.

"Nice to meet you, Astrid," Ginny said. "Draper, I'm going to find Macks and say hello."

"Good. I know she'll be glad you're here," he said. "I'll catch up with you in just a minute."

Before Ginny turned to go, Astrid was already pulling him back into the web of her conversation, leaning in, one hand on his bicep, the other splayed on his chest.

Suddenly, Ginny wanted to go home. It was cool to have her work in this show, and she was appreciative to Macks for including her, but this—she glanced around—this was not her scene.

But Draper was in his element. Ginny cut her gaze in the direction of Draper and Astrid, but the crowd had swallowed them up.

That's when Macks walked by, looking stunning in her flowing white linen top, which hung seductively off one bare shoulder, and wide-legged trousers. She was blond, tanned and beautiful.

"Oh, hi, Macks," Ginny said.

Macks blinked once, then twice, as if she was trying to place Ginny.

"Ginny Sanders from... Austin."

She couldn't bring herself to say "Rambling Rose" after the way Draper had made it sound like a blip on the map. She was probably just being sensitive and reading too much into his words. But she and Macks had met in Austin.

Even so, Ginny felt like she was selling out her hometown.

Mack's face bloomed in recognition. "Oh, yes! Ginny. Draper's girlfriend."

Huh?

"You're here? I'm thrilled you're here. Your paintings arrived yesterday. If I'd known you were coming, you could've just brought them."

That would've been nice. She would've saved the 150 dollars she'd spent on express shipping and insurance, but that didn't matter now.

"Your paintings look great. Have you seen them yet?"

"No, Draper and I just got here."

Someone walked up and said something to Macks that Ginny couldn't hear.

"Okay, I'll take care of it right away," she said.

"Ginny, I'm sorry, I have to run and tend to a matter, but let's catch up later, okay?"

A man who was half-a-head shorter than Macks reached out and grabbed her around the waist as she was starting to walk away.

"Hello, gorgeous," he said.

"Serge! How wonderful to see you. I'm needed over there." Macks gestured to the back of the gallery. "But have you met Ginny Sanders? She's a very talented artist I've just discovered. She has three paintings in the show. Ginny, this is Serge Wilkensen. Sorry, I really have to run. More later."

Ginny wasn't sure to whom Macks was promising

"more later," but the woman was off, leaving Ginny to chat with this man who stared at her breasts for the duration of the stilted conversation. Ginny gave her empty champagne flute to a passing server, crossed her arms over her chest and put one hand on her chin, trying to send the message "Eyes up here, mister." When that didn't work, she excused herself to find her paintings.

Good talk, Serge.

Finally, she found them about three quarters of the way back along the right-hand wall. Seeing her work hanging in the same collection as other talented women artists took her breath away and tears of pride stung her eyes. *This is mine. I did this.* She couldn't wait for Draper to see them. She glanced around the gallery, hoping to pick him out in the crowd and see him walking toward her with more champagne and a smile, but there was no sign of him. At least not from her vantage point.

That green, thorny creature that had hatched when Astrid appeared reared its ugly head again. But Ginny pushed it down. Any girlfriend of Draper Fortune's needed to have a steel girder of confidence. Otherwise, the constant traffic of women who wanted Draper could break her.

The truth was women loved Draper.

The only thing that mattered was who Draper loved.

She could give him some space with Astrid and the memory of Simone, whoever she was. Ginny had a pretty good idea that she was the ghost of a girlfriend past. Or at least someone whose heart Draper had broken.

The green meanie grumbled.

Ignoring it, Ginny took out her cell phone and snapped some photos of her work, then texted them to Kirby. Her friend replied immediately.

Ooooh, look at those! They're beautiful! Get Draper to take a picture of you with them. Then get someone to take a picture of you and Draper. [wink emoji]

Ginny's gaze swept the room again. No Draper.

It had been about twenty minutes since she'd left him to talk to Astrid. Not that she was clocking him, but as with any situation, there was a time frame for talking to someone that was acceptable. Ginny had no idea how many minutes that was. But *acceptable* had just crossed over to *you are neglecting your date.*

Girlfriend or not, he'd brought her here and it was wrong to abandon her.

Kirby texted again: Pics, please.

Ginny snapped a selfie, doing her best to smile through her eyes and cover up the irritation that multiplied exponentially as each minute passed.

As she composed the text to Kirby, a couple walked up to her paintings and stood there. Ginny trained her gaze on her phone but listened intently.

"Good God, they can't really be asking eight hundred and ninety-five dollars a pop for these little paintings?" said the woman.

"What are they?" asked the guy.

"I guess they're supposed to be flowers. Maybe." Ginny looked up to see the woman tilting her head to the side, like a dog desperately trying to understand something.

"Looks like globs of paint. Roger, how long do you think it took to paint these? Maybe fifteen minutes?" The woman snort-laughed. "I mean seriously. I should take up painting if this is what they're passing off for art these days."

White-hot humiliation stung Ginny like a thousand sharp needles. But then something else won out. She loved her flower paintings. How dare this couple with big opinions belittle them.

She sent the selfie to Kirby, but she didn't wait to hear what else the couple had to say. Instead, she pushed her way through the crowd toward the door. She had never felt so alone in the middle of so many people. She had no idea what to do with herself.

As she reached the front door, she saw Draper walking in alone from outside. He waved and joined her.

"Did you find Macks?"

"I did."

I talked to her about as much as I've talked to you tonight.

"Where were you?" she asked, trying to keep accusatory notes out of her voice. "I've been looking for you."

His grimace was almost imperceptible, but she saw it.

She hated looking so needy, so dependent on him, but—

"I walked Astrid to her car."

The thorny, green creature howled and Ginny had to bite the insides of her cheeks to keep the sound from escaping.

Draper was totally in his element and she was utterly out of hers. Back in Rambling Rose, she'd never noticed the crevasse that separated their lives, but on Draper's turf they were miles apart.

That's probably why he was acting…different now.

"Where are your paintings?" he said. "Show me."

"You saw them in Texas," she said. "They look the same here. I just want to go home."

"But we were going to dinner."

When she didn't answer, he said, "I'd at least like to see the rest of the work in the show."

He smiled, and she could tell he way trying. She suddenly felt like the anchor keeping him from having fun.

They walked around and looked at the rest of the artwork, which ranged from paintings and collages, to sculptures and photographs.

The crowd noise made the fact that they weren't saying much to each other less painful. Draper ran into several more friends, but he introduced her as Ginny Sanders, an artist from Texas and kept the conversations short.

By that time, Ginny was too numb to care. This night seemed indicative of how different they were. She'd even fooled herself into believing that she could fake it until it became natural, but the truth was, she did not belong here.

Her place was in Rambling Rose, teaching school and painting flowers on her front porch. That was the only thing she was certain of. Well, that and the fact that she loved her flower paintings. Even if Mr. and Mrs. Big Opinion hated them. She wasn't ashamed that she'd produced the paintings in a half hour. The time limit had made her a better artist. It had helped her get out of her head and loosen her style. Because of that breakthrough, she was able to produce art that was simple, straightforward and unpretentious. Unlike when she pretended to be Cinderella charming the prince. The glass slipper had shattered.

It would never fit now because she would never fit in.

By the time they made it back to where they'd been standing earlier, Draper stifled a yawn.

"I guess we should call it a night," he said.

On the way back to his parents' house, the conversation was stilted and Draper seemed distant. Or maybe she was the one who was distant and stilted. She didn't quite know what to say to him and he wasn't making it any easier.

This "surprise" weekend away had turned out to be a surprise, all right. It was nothing like she'd imagined, but it was her fault for putting too many expectations on it.

As if demanding the last word, a message came through the car's Bluetooth mechanism that turned text into speech read aloud by a computer.

It was a message from Astrid. "Hey, loser, you'd better come to the party tomorrow."

She stated the address.

"Don't make me hunt you down because you know I will."

"You heard her," said Ginny. "If you don't go she'll come and find you. I think you should go."

Draper was quiet a moment, then as he steered the car through the large iron gates at his parents' home, he said, "No. I don't think you'd have a good time."

"I'm sure the invite didn't include a plus-one. I'm going home tomorrow. So you should go to the party."

"Don't be ridiculous," he murmured in a monotone.

She noticed he didn't ask her not to go.

Frankly, she wasn't sure she wanted to spend all day tomorrow with moody, pensive Draper. Tears stung the back of her eyes as she thought about the plastic people at the gallery, and the mean things the couple had said when they were looking at her art.

Art was subjective and people had moods.

She understood this and wished she could talk

to Draper about it—her Draper, not this cranky imposter—but she already felt a little too thin-skinned thanks to the art world. It wasn't a good idea to take off her armor and lay her bruised soul bare to this man who had already taken too much.

The bottom line was, she'd offered herself to Draper and he'd taken it. He hadn't forced himself on her nor made her any promises.

She had assumed.

That things had turned out this way wasn't entirely his fault.

She knew his MO. She knew he sent mixed messages, making women think he was serious when he had no intention of making the relationship permanent. He just couldn't resist a challenge.

Before they'd gotten involved, before she'd let herself believe she was different, that she'd be the one who made the elusive Draper Fortune commit, he'd told her he pushed women away when he felt like they were getting too close.

"You're pushing me away, Draper."

She turned to him, but his face was cloaked in shadow.

"I guess I'm just not ready to get serious with anyone."

His words were a punch to the gut, even though she should've expected them.

Ginny remembered that day when Ines had chucked the chocolates into her yard, as if she'd been passing the mantle. So this was what it felt like to be an Ines, a Natalie, a Simone—a woman who believed she was the only person in Draper Fortune's world, until she fell in love with him and he'd conquered the challenge and had to wriggle free of her grasp.

It was all a game to him.

Now it was her turn to throw the proverbial chocolate.

"I appreciate everything you've done to get me here this weekend, but I'm flying home tomorrow."

Chapter Thirteen

Saturday morning, the sane part of Draper's mind screamed at him to do something—anything—to make Ginny stay.

Don't let her go.

The words ricocheted around his chest in the vicinity of his heart as he carried her suitcase downstairs and listened to her say goodbye to his mother.

Ginny had done a good job of keeping a brave face. She had thanked his mom profusely for her hospitality, saying that something unexpected had come up and she was forced to leave earlier than planned.

Because of the gracious way Ginny left, she gave his mother no clue that he had behaved like a jackass the night before. If Ginny had pitched a fit or informed his mother that she needed to teach him some manners about how to treat a lady, it might have been easier to justify that letting her go was the right thing. But she hadn't behaved that way.

She was perfect.

And he was an idiot.

As they stood outside in the driveway, waiting for her Uber, he managed to utter "Ginny…"

She turned to him. "Draper?"

But he couldn't form the rest of the words he needed to say…the words that mattered. They were stuck in his esophagus.

He knew he would choke on them later. He deserved to choke, because all he could do was stand there silently aching and miserable as he watched her get into the blue Nissan Sentra that carried her out of his life.

That's when he found his voice.

"I'm sorry," he murmured. "I'm so sorry."

Just like that, he'd let her go.

In more ways than one. By not fighting for her to stay, he knew he was letting her walk out of his life as he had so many women in the past.

Only this time it felt different.

He wasn't experiencing that rush of relief that was like a deep breath of pure oxygen when he disengaged. This was confusing. It felt like a hangover after drinking too much. He knew he'd brought it on himself and deserved to feel awful. He should be swearing off the poison—not that Ginny was poison…

On the contrary. She was the antidote.

He was the poison. This shell of a life he was leading. The revolving door of women who came in and out of his life. The way he lied to himself, pretending he was happy when really he didn't feel anything at all.

Well, he hadn't felt anything until he'd met Ginny.

Watching her walk away hurt.

Maybe feeling nothing was better than this ache in his chest.

He wanted to punch a wall, for all the good that would do. He wasn't a violent person, but he hated himself right now. He hated the disconnect, this kill switch that tripped when a woman got too close or demanded too much.

Only, Ginny hadn't asked for anything.

And she was the one who had left him.

A traitorous part of him longed to see her again. No, more than that, he wished they could go back to the way things were before he'd given in to his weakness for her and then let her walk away.

No amount of justification gave him the right to even try to talk to her now. That would be insulting and even more disrespectful than he'd already been to her. Even though he hadn't meant to disrespect her.

Because of that, he was left to thrash around in his own personal hell.

Saturday night he'd had no desire to go to Astrid's party. He wasn't in the mood. Instead, he opted for a low-key night with his parents.

He was hanging out with his mother in the kitchen when he said, "I'm so sorry Ginny had to leave."

Sarah said, "I really like her. Not only is she beautiful, but she's so sweet. I approve."

He'd wanted to punch something earlier, but now her words were a punch in the gut. "It's not like that, Mom."

"Draper, why not? She's a lovely young woman."

She didn't say it, but "Much better than any of the other women you've dated" was strongly implied. So was "What the hell is wrong with you?"

He had been asking himself that same question all day. It had followed him around like a black cloud.

She changed the subject. "Would you please set the table in the dining room?"

"Sure."

When Draper and his six siblings had lived at home, his parents had employed a full-time chef and housekeeper. Now that Sarah and Miles were empty nesters, they had cut back to a once-a-week housekeeper who did the heavy lifting, as Sarah liked to say, and a chef who prepared healthy meals for the two of them. Still, Sarah loved to cook and relished the chance to prepare sumptuous meals for her kids when they were in town or available for dinner. She was famous for her beef Wellington, which she had prepared for tonight's dinner.

As Draper set the table, he noticed Sarah had given him five place settings.

"Who is joining us for dinner tonight?" he asked.

Sarah smiled as she dried her hands on a dish towel. "Austin and Felicity. I'm so happy they were available. They've been so busy. It's been ages since we've seen them."

His brother Austin had been promoted to vice president of Fortune Investments. His wife, Felicity, was the director of advertising. She had gone to college while working full-time as Austin's executive assistant before the two had fallen in love and gotten married.

The fact that they were married was nothing short of a miracle given the catastrophe of Austin's first marriage.

A decade ago, Austin had fallen in love with a woman named Kelly and had eloped with her after knowing her for only two weeks. She turned out to be a con artist.

She'd lied about her identity, claiming to be an heiress. Austin had believed her because she was so convincing and he was in love with her.

A short while later they learned that Austin wasn't her first mark. A guy that Kelly had bamboozled tracked her down and threatened to press charges and expose her.

Their father paid off the guy because Miles didn't want the scandal to ruin the family and the business he'd worked his entire adult life to build.

Despite being a Fortune by name, Miles had built Fortune Investments on his own from the ground up. He was afraid that if the guy pressed charges against

Kelly, Fortune Investments would lose its clients because they wouldn't trust an investment company that had ties to swindlers.

In the end, Austin had gotten a divorce and had to work for years to pay back their father.

The entire night Draper watched Austin and Felicity. They were so clearly in love.

Felicity was beautiful in an understated, natural way—kind of like Ginny.

Something weird twisted in Draper's stomach at the thought.

More important, she was kind and caring, and Austin seemed so happy, compared to the years between Kelly and Felicity, when he'd been a husk of a man.

That was the part that had imprinted on Draper. He couldn't stand seeing his brother, a guy who'd had so much promise, broken by a woman who didn't give a crap about him. All she'd wanted was his money…the family's money.

But look at him now.

"You seem really happy," Draper said to Austin when they were in the process of retiring to the living room for after-dinner brandies.

Austin's smile said it all. "There's nothing like the love of a good woman."

The words jolted Draper because that was exactly what Beau had said about Sofia. Draper had brushed it off as weakness.

He should've expected Austin to utter the same

sentiment, as his brother couldn't take his eyes off Felicity, who had settled on the sofa next to his mother. The two had their heads together, seemingly conspiring about something.

At a break in the conversation, both of them glanced at Draper. He had a sinking feeling that he knew exactly what—or whom—they were talking about.

Ginny's name had been conspicuously absent from the dinner conversation.

Even though thoughts of her had haunted Draper like a specter.

Austin sat down next to his wife and draped an arm around her shoulder. It made Draper think of sitting next to Ginny just before they'd made love.

He swallowed the memory. It stung the back of his throat like bile.

Look at Austin.

He's happy and you're the lonely loser.

It didn't even happen to you, and for some asinine reason you still feel like you need to wear armor... and pay your brother's debt.

And the stupidest part is, there is no debt owed.

What the hell is wrong with you?

That's exactly what he kept asking himself for the next week after he returned to Rambling Rose. He'd messed up everything with Ginny and he didn't know how to fix it.

At first, he distracted himself with work because business was so busy it had him leaving home early in the morning and returning late, long after dark, and after Ginny had finished her daily painting on her front porch. Even so, that didn't stop him from glancing over as he passed her house before turning into his own driveway.

He also occupied his mind with the case of the mysterious gifts that he and his relatives had received.

Today, he and several of the Fortunes had agreed to meet Mariana at Roja to see if they could collectively sort it out. That morning, he'd let Megan know about the record and she promised to procure a way to play it.

Draper was the last to arrive. When he walked into the private dining room, Mariana was seated at the table, along with his twin cousins Brady and Brian and their brother, Josh. Beau and their sister Belle were there and so were their cousins Ashley, Megan and Nicole.

Everyone was noshing on taquitos, empanadas and nachos, compliments of Nicole's culinary expertise.

"It's about time," Beau said when Draper walked in. "We were beginning to think you were a no-show."

"Sorry, everyone, I was held up with a client from Houston," Draper said. "It's been a crazy day."

"Glad you're here," said Brian. "Grab a plate of food and a glass of sangria and let's get down to business."

As Draper helped himself to the food and drink, Brian said, "I know we've all received some strange gifts lately. I thought if we looked at them as a collection, we might be able to figure out how they're connected and what the sender is trying to tell us."

"And who the sender is," said Belle. "That might be the biggest clue of all."

Everyone murmured their agreement.

Brian presented the poem that he found in the Austin Savings Bank safe-deposit box when he used the key he'd found in back of the horse statue that was sent to his brother, Brady. He read it aloud.

"'What is mine is yours. What is yours is mines. I hope you can read between the lines. Love is forever, love never dies. You'll see it, too, when you look in her eyes. MAF.' Does that mean anything to anyone? I can't make any sense of it."

Everyone shook their heads.

"MAF," said Ashley. "Who is MAF?"

"I, for one, hope we can figure that out," Belle said. "Because I think it's the same person who sent me this framed painting of the rose, with this inscription—'A rose by any other name would smell as sweet. MAF.'"

"So this MAF authored the poem and painted the picture?" asked Nicole. "What about the blankets? Do they say MAF?"

"The one I received only has an *F* embroidered on it," said Beau.

"Same," said Mariana.

They both placed their identical pink blankets in the middle of the table.

"I brought over that photo of Mariana's mom

that's been hanging in Provisions," Megan said as she set it on the table next to the blankets.

Everyone leaned in to look at the photo.

"It's hard to tell if the blankets we received are the same because of the color quality of the photo, but they do look similar," Mariana said.

The group was quiet for a moment, but it was clear that the collective wheels were turning.

Draper wiped his mouth with the cloth napkin that was in his lap. "The only thing I can see that all of the mysterious items have in common is they contain the letter *F*… *F* for Fortune, presumably, since we're all getting the gifts and we're all Fortunes."

"Well, except for me," said Mariana. "As far as we know anyway. But my mother had the blanket with an *F* on it in that photo."

She looked like she wanted to say more, but she stopped.

"What, Mariana?" asked Nicole.

Mariana waved away her question. "Nah, it's nothing. Go on. Are there any more weird gifts?"

"I have one," Draper said. "But it's a curveball because not only does it not have an *F* or an *MAF* stamped on it, but I don't even know what it is other than it's an old record. Megan, were you able to get a record player?"

"Absolutely. I set it up over in the corner away from the food and drinks."

Draper took the album out of the cover. Gripping it by its edges, he held it up so the others could get a look. "See, it's a record, but it has no label. The jacket was completely blank, too."

"Maybe the music isn't as important as what the album stands for," said Brian. "Could it be some sort of secret message?"

"But what could it be?" asked Josh.

Draper switched on the stereo. As he set the album on the turntable, his mind flashed to kissing Ginny the night the record was delivered. For a nanosecond, Draper's heart bloomed, but then the reality of where they stood crashed down, weighty and dark. It held him under. His need for her was like a drowning person desperate for air.

He tried to blink away the anguish as he lowered the arm onto the record.

At first they heard scratches and skips, the sound of old vinyl under a needle. Then there was the sound of maracas and an instrumental song played in lo-fi quality.

"Okay..." Ashley shrugged. "I don't get it. What is that song?"

"It's calypso music." Mariana closed her eyes and listened. "I don't know what it's called, but it sounds familiar."

Everyone was squinting and scowling as they listened hard. Some were bobbing their heads to the music, looking confused as they tried to draw a common thread from the poem to the picture to the blankets, which all had an *F* or *MAF*...and then there was this song. An old calypso song with no obvious significance. The music was cheerful, anyway, so they kept it on as they continued to talk.

Then Mariana began to hum along.

With her eyes closed, she leaned forward and put her palms on the table as she kept humming. When she opened her eyes, she looked a little pale. "I know this song. There's a memory here, but I can't quite— Wait a minute—I think my mom used to sing it to me when I was a baby. The words are something about the shifting sands by the sea." She pressed her hand to her forehead. "Why can't I remember?"

A guy from the kitchen came into the dining room and started collecting the plates from the table. As he worked, he moved his shoulders to the music and began to sing about a woman named Mary Ann sifting sand by the sea. "'All the children love—'"

"Lee, what did you say?" Mariana sat up ramrod straight in her chair.

Lee's hand flew to his mouth. "Sorry, I didn't mean to interrupt."

"You're not interrupting," said Draper. "We've been trying to figure out what this song is called."

"It's something like Mary Ann. I'm not one hundred percent sure, but it goes like this…"

Lee began singing along with the instrumental music and everyone froze.

Mariana's eyes grew large and her hands flew to her mouth.

"Mary Ann… Mariana." She lowered her hands

and scanned the Fortunes seated at the table. "Could MAF be Mary Ann Fortune?"

"'You'll see it, too, when you look in her eyes,'" murmured Brian, alluding to the poem.

Everyone turned and looked at Mariana.

"She does resemble some of us a little," Nicole said.

"Why has no one ever noticed this before?" Ashley asked.

"Mariana, let's say that is your mother in the photo with the blanket," Draper said. "Can you tell us about your family?"

"Sadly, I never knew my father," Mariana said. "But I have to admit since seeing the picture on the wall in Provisions in context with the blankets that Beau and I received, if it is my mother, I have wondered about her ancestry. I know this might be a stretch, but do you think she could've been related to the Fortunes?"

They all sat looking at each other, and Draper was nearly certain that they were thinking what he was thinking—that given the way the Fortune family had been expanding over the last five years, it wasn't so far-fetched an idea.

Mariana must've mistaken their silence for negativity. "I know it's unlikely, but given all the clues we have here, I think someone might be trying to tell us something."

"Looks that way," said Belle.

"I wish I had relatives who could tell me about

my past," Mariana said. "Unfortunately, my mother is deceased, and I don't know of any other blood relatives."

"You're absolutely right about someone wanting us Fortunes to make the connection," Draper said. "But who? And why now, after all these years? I'm with you, Mariana. It's becoming a question that I think we all want answered."

"One way we could get at least some answers is if you take a DNA test," Megan suggested. "If you were open to it."

Everyone nodded.

"I think it's important," said Belle. "I mean, we could be related."

"I'll do it, if you all think it would be helpful in solving this gift mystery." Mariana's eyes filled with tears. "Besides... Do you know what it would mean to me to finally find my family after all these years?"

Draper couldn't wait to tell Ginny what they'd discovered. Even though they weren't on the best of terms right now, she deserved to know since she was the one who first drew the connection between the blanket and the photo in Provisions, and she'd been there when the album was delivered.

Once again, the memory of the kiss flooded through him. The way she'd felt, the way they'd fit together like two puzzle pieces, and not just when they'd made love. The way she was the first person he wanted to talk to when he learned about things like this.

Even more important than losing a lover was that he had lost his best friend.

After the way he'd treated her, he didn't deserve her, but she deserved to know. She might spit in his face—as if she would do something like that—but she needed to hear this from him before word got out, as it inevitably would.

Draper parked and went next door. He rang Ginny's doorbell, but Jerry answered the door, and he didn't look happy.

"What do you want, Fortune?"

"Hey, Jerry, I need to talk to Ginny."

"She doesn't want to talk to you. Frankly, I don't blame her after the way you treated her, like she's some disposable bimbo. I don't care if you're a rich and powerful Fortune—" He waved away the words as if the surname was stinking up the place. "You're not worthy of my sister. Just leave her alone."

Jerry shut the door in Draper's face.

Draper stood there for a minute, trying to think about what to do, but he finally decided Jerry was right. He wasn't worthy of Ginny.

With an aching heart, he turned to go. When he reached the bottom of the steps, he heard the door squeak open.

"What do you want, Draper?" Ginny said.

He turned and saw her standing there looking more beautiful than he'd ever seen her, in jeans and a Madonna concert T-shirt, her face scrubbed free of makeup and her hair piled upon her head in a messy knot.

It felt like his heart leaped from his body, out onto the sidewalk, and bounced around several times before it slammed back into his chest leaving him breathless.

"Ginny…" It was all he could manage to say.

"Gin, what are you doing?" Jerry was back. "You don't have to talk to that SOB."

"I know I don't," she said, "I'll be fine. Could you please give us some privacy?"

Ten days.

It took him ten days to get in touch after what happened in New Orleans.

Draper probably thought she would come and find him. Seek him out, like the other women in his life usually did. Ginny hadn't done that, of course. Not that she deserved a medal for bravery. If she'd been strong, she wouldn't be standing on her porch, trying to swallow down the tangle of weakness and angst as she watched him stew on the walkway below.

Ten days.

Remember that...and how he acted in New Orleans.

That saying about when someone shows you who they are, you should believe them seemed particularly relevant right now. She would make it her mantra.

"What do you want, Draper?" she asked again.

A frown slowly eclipsed the smile he'd been wearing when she'd first appeared, but then he schooled his face into a neutral expression.

"Interesting news," he said and told her about the discoveries they'd made at the family meeting—about the record being the calypso tune "Mary Ann," which made them believe that all the mysterious gifts pointed toward Mariana being part of the Fortune family. "I thought you'd want to know."

Ginny nodded. "I hope this turns out well for Mariana."

She started to add "after all, the Fortune family does have a reputation for taking what they want and discarding the extraneous." But her better angels stopped her. She knew that even though Draper had hurt her, it wasn't fair to paint the entire family with the same broad brush.

As a whole, the Fortunes were good people who had made a difference in Rambling Rose.

It was her own fault for letting Draper close enough to take advantage of her.

Something else stirred deep inside of her, suggesting he wasn't solely to blame, that it took two to tango, free will, blah, blah, blah…but right now, she needed to blame him so she didn't backpedal right back into his arms.

Draper shifted from one foot to another and cleared his throat. "I know what you're saying. None of us wants Mariana to get hurt. She volunteered to take a DNA test before we talk about anything else."

"Mariana's a sweetheart," Ginny said. "I wish her only good things. Thanks for letting me know, Draper."

She turned to go back inside.

"Ginny, I know I was a jerk in New Orleans and I'm sorry," Draper said. "Please don't judge my entire family on my actions."

She turned around and looked him square in the eyes. "Oh, I won't do that. You can count on it."

When she put her hand on the knob, he said, "Ginny, I value your friendship more than I can say."

Ginny winced. Wow. Was friendship supposed to be a consolation prize? *I took you for a test drive and decided, naaah, but let's still be friends because I want everyone to like me.*

"Okay, Draper," she said in a monotone. She left off the word *whatever*, but made sure that it was implied.

"Ginny, that didn't come out right." In her peripheral vision, she saw him shake his head. "I'm messing up again. Yes, I value your friendship, but the best relationships are built on a solid foundation of friendship. I know I haven't given you much reason to like me lately. But I hope you'll let me make it up to you. Somehow."

In the midst of his monologue on friendship, Ginny had turned toward him, unsure of where he was going, but waiting for him to say something that would change her mind, but all he talked about was friendship. *The best relationships are built on a solid foundation of friendship?* Okay, whatever that meant. The "friend" ship had already sailed and he'd jumped overboard when he—they'd—gotten too close.

"What are you trying to say, Draper? Why do you want to be my friend? You made it clear you're not staying in Rambling Rose. It's obvious that I don't fit into your New Orleans world. I don't want to end up being like Astrid or Simone. How was that party, by the way? Did you have fun?"

She shouldn't have stooped to sarcasm. It exposed her, made him know she still cared.

"I didn't go."

She raised her eyebrows, not wanting to believe him. But he'd never lied to her. If anything, he'd been too truthful.

"After you left, I wasn't exactly in the mood for a party."

"Sorry to spoil your good time."

She had so many questions. Did he see Astrid again? Did Simone get a chance to throw a drink in his face? What exactly happened between him and Simone?

No! No. No. No. No.

None of it mattered.

"You didn't spoil my good time," he said. "I don't know what was wrong with me. I think I was trying to process my feelings. You've made me see things differently. I needed time to sort things out."

"What do you mean?"

She had an idea of what he meant, but she wanted to hear him say it. She wasn't about to jump to conclusions.

"I mean, I... Um, I'm... You're not like the others, Ginny."

She nodded. "You're right about that."

She resisted the urge to say more, to prod him into a confession that didn't come from his heart.

Why was falling in love with someone so hard?

Unless that wasn't want he wanted at all.

They stood there in excruciating silence staring at each other, but he didn't say anything else.

In fact, he looked pained, like he wanted to crawl under a rock.

Finally, it hit her. The only reason he wanted her now was because he couldn't have her. She was worth more than being his challenge.

The irony was she owed at least part of her newfound self-worth to him.

After Trey had raped her, she'd believed she was damaged goods. She felt unlovable because she'd believed what had happened was somehow her fault. But it wasn't her fault.

Draper had taught her that she had to love herself before anyone else could love her. It hadn't been easy, but now she finally believed that wherever Trey Hartnet was in this world, he would get exactly what he deserved. Somewhere, somehow.

She wasn't going to worry about it anymore.

Now was her time to live the life she deserved.

Because of Draper, Ginny knew she could feel again. She was capable of loving and allowing herself to be loved. Someday she would find love, and until then, she was worth more than being someone's challenge. She was a living, breathing human being who possessed talents and feelings that were not defined or diminished by how a man treated her or felt about her.

But it was up to her to make sure she was treated well.

Some men took what they wanted however they could get it—by force or by charm—and then they threw it away like yesterday's news. Ginny would never let a man toss her away again. Though it hurt to walk away from Draper. Next time she gave herself, it would be to a man who would love her forever.

"Draper, right now I'm a challenge to you."

"That's not true, Ginny."

She held out her hand like a cop stopping traffic. "You'll forget about me soon enough. In the meantime, let's do each other a favor and go on with our lives…separately."

Draper looked crestfallen, but it wasn't her problem.

She went inside and shut the door.

For the second time in ten days, Draper watched Ginny walk away. Only this time, he was determined to prove she wasn't just a challenge. His feelings for her were real. Even if he was having a difficult time articulating them.

He was in love with her.

He'd never felt this way about a woman.

He needed a minute to figure out what to do with those feelings so he didn't mess this up—again.

He had to fight the impulse to go pound on her door again and try to make her listen to him, but wouldn't that just reinforce her thoughts that he was just in this to conquer a challenge?

Instead, he would give her a little time—not too much, though—while he came up with a plan to make her see how much she meant to him.

"Miss Sanders, could you please come to the office during your planning period? Mrs. Glass would like a word." The summons came over the intercom in her classroom, scratchy but loud.

"Absolutely," Ginny said, over the taunts of her third period American lit class.

"Ooh, Miss Sanders has to go to the principal's office," a chorus of voices sang in unison. "Somebody's in trouble."

"Settle down, please. No one's in trouble, but you are going to get extra homework if you don't stop this nonsense."

Ginny forced a smile and wished she could calm her nerves as fast as her class settled down. The problem was, she had a sinking feeling she *was* in trouble. That dread was confirmed when she saw the dozens upon dozens of sunflowers that transformed the receptionist's desk into something that resembled a Tuscan field.

"More flowers?" she asked Julie, the school receptionist, who was barely visible through the sea of yellow and brown.

For the third day in a row, she'd received an enormous bouquet delivered to school. And they weren't your average FTD specials. They were from Draper and they were so large, they looked like they belonged in a palace or a hotel lobby—the first day it was roses, the second day it was lilies, today the sunflowers had arrived.

"Julie, I am so sorry," Ginny said.

"I don't mind. But Mrs. Glass thanks this is getting a little ridiculous. But forget about that—how long have you been dating Draper Fortune? He is so gorgeous."

Obviously, she'd peeked at the cards, which, thank goodness, hadn't said anything scandalous, just versions of "I can't stop thinking of you" and "When can I see you?"

Ginny started to tell her she wasn't dating Draper Fortune, but Mrs. Glass appeared in the doorway. "Ginny, come in," she said brusquely.

When they entered her office, the principal didn't even ask her to sit down.

"I'll keep this brief because I know you have work to do on your planning period, but you must ask your boyfriend to stop with the flowers. He can't send them to the school. Once in a while is fine, if it's a birthday or a special anniversary, but every day is too much. It's disruptive. We're all happy that you've found a man who adores you, but you must ask him to contain his amorous enthusiasm to after school hours. It's setting a bad example."

Ginny's ears burned. What she really wanted was to melt into the floorboards.

Not only would the entire town of Rambling Rose know that there had been something between Draper and her, but they'd also know that she'd gotten fired if he didn't stop this nonsense.

This proved that they really did live in different worlds.

After school, she dropped off the sunflowers at the local nursing home, just as she had with the roses and lilies. She waited for Draper to get home so she could go next door and ask him to stop. But if she thought the flowers were excessive, the diamond earrings that were delivered from Hill's Jewelers in downtown Rambling Rose were the last straw.

Thank goodness Jerry wasn't home when they came that afternoon. Because if he had been, he would've insisted on returning the earrings to Draper for her and she would've had to come up with a reason why she needed to do this herself. She couldn't articulate why she needed to do it.

She just needed to.

The minute Draper's car pulled into the driveway

she marched over with the small red velvet box and pounded on his door.

His face lit up when he answered and saw her standing there, but it fell when she held out the earrings. “Please stop sending me gifts.”

“If you’d rather have pearls or something else, we can exchange them,” he said.

“Draper, I asked you to stop.”

His smile faded.

“I got called into the principal’s office today because of all the flowers. If you won’t listen to me, my principal is asking you to stop. I got in trouble, okay?”

“I’m sorry,” he said. “Would you like to come in?”

“No.” She held out the small box again. “I just came over to give this back and to beg you to not send me anything else.”

Looking reluctant, he accepted the jewelry. “There’s something that’s going to be delivered tomorrow. It’s too late to stop it.”

“Not to school. Please tell me you haven’t sent it to school.”

“No, it’s coming to the house.”

“Well, I’ll be bringing it back, too.”

“It’s something that I think you’ll like.” His words were hopeful. “You’ll like it more than diamonds. I knew in my heart these weren’t you. I should’ve listened to my heart.”

She sighed. “Draper, I am not like the material girls you’ve dated in the past. You can’t buy me with bling. Or even with flowers. And if you can't figure it out, then..." She shrugged. "Then there's no hope for us."

"When I do figure it out," he said, "does that mean there's a chance for us?"

Chapter Fourteen

Draper knew that in the world of sales, "no" never meant "absolutely not."

It could mean "not now," but more often, it meant "convince me."

If you were worth your salt in the sales world, an objection was something to be overcome, something to be turned into a "yes." You just had to listen for the key words that were clues to converting the client from a negative to a positive.

Sitting alone in his office, he thought about how when Ginny had returned the earrings, she'd said she couldn't be bought with bling or flowers. If he couldn't figure it out…then there was no hope for them.

He needed to figure out what "it" was. He knew

she was not swayed by gifts. He'd had an easel she'd talked about and the most expensive set of artist-quality paints delivered to her house yesterday. He'd found them on his porch that evening. This time she hadn't even rung the bell.

She didn't respond to practical gifts. Nor did flowers and jewelry seem to influence her, which made her a unicorn among the women he always attracted. What woman didn't love diamonds?

The rocks he'd sent were for her ears, of course. The diamond ring would come later—

The thought startled him. That he was even thinking about an engagement ring made him freeze up, like one of those myotonic goats that was struck with paralysis when frightened.

He took a deep breath and exhaled slowly.

Engagement ring aside, the stunned goat impression that had happened to him when they were in New Orleans. He'd witnessed with his own eyes the contrast between Ginny and the world that used to be his, and it paralyzed him because it was no contest that Ginny was not only the woman he should be with…but she was also the woman he wanted.

But that meant giving up everything else.

By the time Saturday evening had rolled around back in NOLA a few weekends ago, he'd realized he had no desire to go to a party and hook up with Simone or start something up with Astrid, because that's what she'd been offering. He could pretend like she had solely been looking out for Simone and facilitating their reconciliation, but Draper had been in that exact situation too many times to try and pretend like it was anything else than what it was. The Astrids, the Simones, the Natalies, the Ineses—they were all cut from the same cloth.

Just like the woman who had taken his own brother, Austin, for a ride and cost his family millions of dollars and unspeakable humiliation. After Austin went through it, Draper swore he would never let it happen to him. There must've been something inside of him that tempted him into situations that took him right up to the edge. Date the fancy women, but prove that he was stronger than that. That he was better than that.

And to what end? So that he ended up pushing away every woman who got too close?

Thank God, he'd realized that before it was too late and he lost Ginny for good.

But he still had work to do. He needed to figure out what it was she wanted and prove to her that they deserved a chance to be happy together.

Never one to try to go it alone, Draper figured the best and fastest way to get to the bottom of this was to talk to someone who knew her best. He called Kirby and asked her if he could take her to lunch and pick her brain about all things Ginny.

Seated at Provisions, Draper launched into the history of Draper and Ginny. He didn't mince words or try to gloss over the times that he'd behaved like a jackass—or goat—or any number of barnyard animals that couldn't get out of their own way.

"I know what I've done wrong," he said. "I just can't figure out what I can do to make it right. How can I make Ginny believe I love her?"

Kirby blinked at him. "You're really in love with her? Like really in love with her?"

"I am," he said, waiting for the goat paralysis to kick in, but it didn't. This time he was solidly standing on his own feet.

"You know she's convinced that you're in this for the challenge?" Kirby said before biting into a french fry. She chewed and swallowed. "You need to do some soul-searching, Draper, and figure out if she's really what you want. She's small-town Rambling Rose not big-city NOLA, not that she couldn't visit and adapt very well. She's a special woman and the guy who does get her is going to be very lucky."

Draper nodded.

Kirby blotted the corners of her mouth with her napkin, then looked Draper square in the eyes. "She's been through a lot. She told me she confided in you about what happened."

Kirby was silent for a few beats, as if letting the words sink in.

Draper swallowed hard at the thought of what it meant that Ginny had trusted him with her secret.

"She's not playing at this," Kirby said. "If this is a game to you, then you need to get up right now and leave."

"It's not a game. For the first time in my life, I'm

in love. In the past, I've had feelings for women, but nothing like this."

"Which is probably why it scares you."

Sobered by the depth of his feelings, he nodded. "I love Ginny. I've never been so sure about anything in my entire life."

"You know, this isn't that hard to figure out," she said. "If you can't figure this out for yourself, maybe you don't know her as well as you should."

Of course, her best friend was going to make him work for this. And there was nothing wrong with that. Anything worth having was worth working for.

He shrugged. "I'm sure it's not hard, or at least, it shouldn't be this complicated. But I'll be honest, I'm at a loss here, Kirby. I don't want to lose her." He sat back in his chair.

"Draper, first you need to stop trying to buy her love, and you need to tell her how you feel."

"I have told her how I feel."

"You've told her you're in love with her?" She gave him the side-eye.

He opened his mouth to answer but stopped. "I guess I haven't. Not in those exact words."

"Well." Kirby shrugged with both of her palms up in the air. "You do realize offering gifts is not the same as offering you heart?"

Something shifted in him signaling a glimmer of hope.

Kirby must've seen the light bulb go off, because she said, "Maybe 'I love you' is a good place to start."

* * *

Over the course of the next week, Draper called Ginny every evening, saying he wasn't going to give up.

She had to give him credit. He'd stopped trying to buy her back with gifts, asking instead if he could take her out or at least talk to her. She didn't return his call, though she was tempted when he told her he'd read *Wuthering Heights*.

"Let's not be Cathy and Heathcliff. It's clear that their love was driven by pride and fear. That's no way to be."

He almost had her.

Love?

Let's not be Cathy and Heathcliff.

"He ruined it with 'Let's be Cinderella and Prince Charming, instead,'" Ginny said to Kirby on Saturday morning, when she stopped in for coffee and a chat. "I'm not going to be anyone's Cinderella. Pretty dresses and fancy coaches aside, the story says she's stuck in a subpar life unless the rich guy saves her."

Looking dubious, Kirby shrugged, and it surprised Ginny, who thought her best friend would stand up and cheer her independence.

"What?" Ginny asked.

"I hear what you're saying—you don't need anyone to save you. But be careful not to become so hardened that you spend your life alone."

Ginny's eyes widened, but it was nothing compared to her astonishment when Kirby went on to tell her that she'd had lunch with Draper earlier that week.

"The guy is lovesick," she said.

"No, he's not. He's challenge-sick because he's not getting what he wants. He doesn't love me and that's the point."

"Oh, but he does," Kirby said. "He told me he's in love with you."

White noise roared in Ginny's ears.

"Why didn't you tell me this before now?"

"Because I wanted the two of you to work it out on your own. I had no idea you could be so stubborn."

"Hey, whose side are you on?" Ginny asked.

"I'm on the side of you not losing the love of your life."

Well, that certainly put things into a different perspective.

All day Saturday, Ginny kept going back and forth about what to do. She could call him and tell him he could come over, but it felt too after-the-fact for that. She could go knock on his door, but he hadn't been home all day.

She worked at her easel on the front porch, painting the pink peonies she'd picked up from Petunia's Posies. Not because they reminded her of the bouquet that Draper had given her that time he'd surprised her with flowers, but because they were her favorite.

And she needed something fresh and fun to paint.

Even if they did make her think of Draper...

She'd made herself focus on the day's canvas until

it was completed, rather than fragmenting her flow by glancing over at his driveway every fifteen seconds. When he wasn't home by the time she had finished her painting and cleaned up her mess, her hopes began to wane.

With one last glance at his empty driveway before she went inside, she wondered if it was too late. Had she pushed him away one too many times?

If that was the case, then maybe he didn't really love her after all.

Later that evening, as Ginny and Jerry were working together cleaning up the dinner dishes—Ginny washing and rinsing, Jerry drying and putting away—Jerry stopped and gave Ginny a funny look.

"What is that sound?" he asked. "Do you hear it?"

Ginny switched off the faucet after rinsing the final plate.

"I don't hear anything," she said.

But wait…yes, she did. It was the faint sound of music.

"Where is it coming from?" she asked.

"Outside," Jerry said. "Sounds like someone is having a party and playing music really loud."

Well, it was a Saturday night, though it was unusual for the neighbors to get loud without forewarning. Ginny remembered the party Draper's friend Astrid tried to talk him into and wondered if maybe he had friends over.

Grabbing a dishtowel, she dried her hands. As

she followed Jerry into the living room, the music grew louder. It sounded like it was in her front yard.

She opened the front door and realization dropped like a lead ball, taking her stomach down to her toes.

Draper was standing in her front yard holding a boom box over his head that was blasting "In Your Eyes," just like Lloyd Dobler had done in *Say Anything...* Rattled and afraid that the music would disturb the neighbors, Ginny ran out onto the porch. Her first impulse was to ask him to turn it down, but before she could, he did just that.

"Ginny, I get it," he called. "I finally understand. The most valuable thing I can offer you is my heart. This is me not only offering you my heart, but also my love. I love you, Ginny."

Ginny's hands flew to her mouth and her heart was so full it overflowed, making tears fall from her eyes.

She didn't know what to say or what to do.

She didn't know if he was serious or if this was just another grand gesture designed to conquer the challenge that her attention had become.

Then again, she'd not only refused the expensive gifts he'd offered as a token of his love, but she also hadn't even responded to his subtler means of reaching out, asking if she'd at least talk to him.

This loud, showy demonstration had gotten her attention. It had also brought out the neighbors, who were standing on their porches staring at them, no doubt wondering what all the commotion was about.

Maybe it was time to hear what Draper had to say.

She motioned for him to come up on the porch.

When he did, he stood there looking just as lovesick as Kirby had said he appeared the day he'd talked to her.

"I don't have a ring," he said. "I wanted to give you the chance to pick one out. I didn't want to mess up again."

Ginny knew the subtext was that he didn't want it to be too showy or too small—after all, Draper Fortune was all about grand gestures—but all of a sudden, in this context, that part of his personality seemed generous and sincere.

But what had changed?

When they were in New Orleans, she was his friend Ginny. Rambling Rose was a small, boring town that he wasn't sure he could stomach.

"Let's sit down," she said and motioned for Jerry, who looked like he was ready to fight Draper, to go inside.

"I'll be right here. Let me know if you need me," he said, which probably meant he would be inside trying to listen, the same way that the neighbors were now craning their necks trying to hear what was going on.

When Draper and Ginny sat down on the porch swing, it made it harder for everyone to see unless they dared walk up to her sidewalk. No one she knew would be that brazen.

She hoped.

They sat in silence for a few minutes before Draper said, "Ginny, I love you. It took losing you to finally make me take a long hard look at myself, at my life. I asked myself why I was doing what I was doing. On separate occasions, both Beau and my mom pointed out that I've been dating the wrong women. After our trip to New Orleans, I had to figure out why I was doing that."

He paused.

"That seems to be the million-dollar question, Draper. I've wondered the same thing myself."

"It's kind of a long story."

"I have all night," Ginny said.

Draper sighed. "Where to start… Okay… I always looked up to my oldest brother, Austin. Aside from my dad, he was the smartest guy I'd ever met. I wanted to be just like him."

He told her about Kelly the con artist taking advantage of Austin and their family.

Ginny's jaw dropped. "That sounds like something from a movie."

Draper nodded and shrugged.

"Being a Fortune isn't always what it's cracked up to be. A lot of people only want to know you because of your name and what they think you can do for them."

Ginny grimaced and shook her head.

"I guess what my brother went through and all the family turmoil it caused did more of a number on me than I realized."

"I'm so sorry that happened to your family," Ginny said.

They sat quietly for a moment as she tried to process things. It was so contrary to her way of life, her way of thinking, that it was hard to wrap her mind around the fact that some people had no problem using others to get what they wanted.

Her heart broke a little for Draper.

"That Saturday in New Orleans, instead of going to Astrid's party, I had dinner with my family. Austin and his wife, Felicity, came over. So, yes, even after all he went through, he eventually met someone great. In fact, after I thought about it, I realized Felicity reminds me a lot of you. She's down to earth and such a great, loving person.

"I saw how happy Austin and Felicity are. I realized I had a lot of soul-searching to do to figure out why I go after women who are exactly the type I swore I'd never fall for. After watching my brother nearly destroyed by greed, I guess I wanted to prove that would never happen to me. It was easy to keep women with impure intentions at arm's length because I could see right through them. I realized that what started out as parameters to keep myself from falling for the wrong woman became a challenge to prove to myself that I was impervious to their charms."

"Oh, a challenge, huh? Uh-huh." Ginny pointed at him with her two index fingers.

My point exactly.

"You're right," he said. "I'll be honest, what you said to me the other night—that I only wanted you because you were a challenge to me—made me see it. But I also saw that I was pushing you away—not because you were like the others, but because you are pretty darn perfect for me. You're everything I never knew I wanted. Please tell me I didn't blow it. Will you forgive me?"

Overcome with emotion, Ginny drew in a shuddering breath. "I'm not perfect, Draper. Believe me."

He reached out and with his thumb swiped away a tear that was meandering down her cheek. "You are perfect for me. And I'd be an idiot if I let the woman I love get away. I don't want to lose you, Ginny. I've never been this sure of anything in my entire life."

Draper dropped down on one knee and took her hand in his.

Her heart nearly leapt out of her body. She was so overcome with joy, it felt like shooting stars were coursing through her blood.

"I love you. Will you marry me?"

"Honey, if you won't marry him, I will," called Mrs. Murphy, Ginny's other next-door neighbor.

Ginny's trembling hand flew to her mouth and she made an I'm-sorry face to Draper. What he'd shared was so personal and not meant for others.

But Draper smiled and shrugged, indicating that it was no big deal.

"Mrs. Murphy, I love this woman," Draper called. "I want her to be my wife."

"I can see that, honey. She's the idiot if she says no."

"Will you please put the guy out of his misery?" said Jerry from the other side of the front door. "Say yes, already."

Draper smiled at Ginny, who hiccupped a sob and hid her face in her hands.

Finally, when she couldn't contain her joy any longer, she said, "Yes! I'll marry you."

As the neighbors cheered, Ginny fell into Draper's arms, and they lost themselves in a kiss that made Fourth of July fireworks seem like a backyard sparkler by comparison.

* * * * *

Look for the next book in the new
Harlequin Special Edition continuity
The Fortunes of Texas: The Wedding Gift

A Fortune in the Family
by Kathy Douglass

On sale May 2022 wherever Harlequin books and ebooks are sold.

And catch up with the previous titles in
The Fortunes of Texas: The Wedding Gift

Their New Year's Beginning
by USA TODAY *bestselling author Michelle Major*

A Soldier's Dare
by Jo McNally

Anyone But a Fortune
by USA TODAY *bestselling author Judy Duarte*

Available now, wherever Harlequin books and ebooks are sold.

COMING NEXT MONTH FROM

HARLEQUIN

SPECIAL EDITION

#2905 SUMMONING UP LOVE

Heart & Soul • by Synithia Williams

Vanessa Steele's retreated to her grandmother's beach house after she loses her job and her fiancé. When she finds out her grandmother has enlisted hunky Dion Livingston and his brothers to investigate suspicious paranormal activity, the intrepid reporter's skeptical of their motives. But her own investigation discovers that Dion's the real deal. And any supernatural energy? Pales compared to the electricity that erupts when the two of them are together...

#2906 A FORTUNE IN THE FAMILY

The Fortunes of Texas: The Wedding Gift • by Kathy Douglass

Contractor Josh Fortune is happy to be Kirby Harris's Mr. Fixit. Repairing the roof of Kirby's Perks is a cinch, but healing her heart is a trickier process. For three years the beautiful widow has been doing everything on her own, and she's afraid to let down her guard. She thinks Josh is too young, too carefree—and way too tempting for a mama who has to put her kids first...

#2907 SECOND-CHANCE SUMMER

Gallant Lake Stories • by Jo McNally

For golf pro Quinn Walker, Gallant Lake Resort's cheery yet determined manager, Julie Brown, is a thorn in his side. But the widowed single dad begrudgingly agrees to teach his sassy coworker the game he loves. As their lessons progress, Julie disarms Quinn in ways he can't explain...or ignore. A second chance at love is as rare as a hole in one. Can these rivals at work tee it up for love?

#2908 THE BOOKSHOP RESCUE

Furever Yours • by Rochelle Alers

Lucy Tucker never imagined how dramatically life would change once she started fostering Buttercup, a pregnant golden retriever. The biggest change? Growing a lot closer to Calum Ramsey. One romantic night later, and they're expecting a baby of their own! Stunned at first, steadfastly single Calum is now dutifully offering marriage. But Lucy wants the true-blue happy ending they both deserve.

#2909 A RANCH TO COME HOME TO

Forever, Texas • by Marie Ferrarella

Alan White Eagle hasn't returned to Forever since he left for college eight years ago. But when a drought threatens the town's existence, the irrigation engineer vows to help. An unlikely ally appears in the form of his childhood nemesis, Raegan. In fact, their attraction is challenging Alan's anti-romance workaholic facade. Will Alan's plan to save Forever's future end with a future with Raegan?

#2910 RELUCTANT ROOMMATES

Sierra's Web • by Tara Taylor Quinn

Living with a total stranger for twelve months is the only way Weston Thomas can claim possession of his Georgia family mansion. If not, the place goes to the dogs—seven rescue pups being looked after by Paige Martinson, his co-owner. But when chemistry deepens into more powerful emotions, is the accountant willing to bank on a future that was never in his long-term plans?

SPECIAL EXCERPT FROM

HQN

Mariella Jacob was one of the world's premier bridal designers. One viral PR disaster later, she's trying to get her torpedoed career back on track in small-town Magnolia, North Carolina. With a second-hand store and a new business venture helping her friends turn the Wildflower Inn into a wedding venue, Mariella is finally putting at least one mistake behind her. Until that mistake—in the glowering, handsome form of Alex Ralsten—moves to Magnolia too…

Read on for a sneak preview of Wedding Season, *the next book in* USA TODAY *bestselling author Michelle Major's Carolina Girls series!*

"You still don't belong here." Mariella crossed her arms over her chest, and Alex commanded himself not to notice her body, perfect as it was.

"That makes two of us, and yet here we are."

"I was here first," she muttered. He'd heard the argument before, but it didn't sway him.

"You're not running me off, Mariella. I needed a fresh start, and this is the place I've picked for my home."

"My plan was to leave the past behind me. You are a physical reminder of so many mistakes I've made."

"I can't say that upsets me too much," he lied. It didn't make sense, but he hated that he made her so uncomfortable. Hated even more that sometimes he'd purposely drive by

PHMMEXP0322

her shop to get a glimpse of her through the picture window. Talk about a glutton for punishment.

She let out a low growl. “You are an infuriating man. Stubborn and callous. I don’t even know if you have a heart.”

“Funny.” He kept his voice steady even as memories flooded him, making his head pound. “That’s the rationale Amber gave me for why she cheated with your fiancé. My lack of emotions pushed her into his arms. What was his excuse?”

She looked out at the street for nearly a minute, and Alex wondered if she was even going to answer. He followed her gaze to the park across the street, situated in the center of the town. There were kids at the playground and several families walking dogs on the path that circled the perimeter. Magnolia was the perfect place to raise a family.

If a person had the heart to be that kind of a man—the type who married the woman he loved and set out to be a good husband and father. Alex wasn’t cut out for a family, but he liked it in the small coastal town just the same.

“I was too committed to my job,” she said suddenly and so quietly he almost missed it.

“Ironic since it was your job that introduced him to Amber.”

“Yeah.” She made a face. “This is what I’m talking about, Alex. A past I don’t want to revisit.”

“Then stay away from me, Mariella,” he advised. “Because I’m not going anywhere.”

“Then maybe I will,” she said and walked away.

SPECIAL EXCERPT FROM

HARLEQUIN

SPECIAL EDITION

For golf pro Quinn Walker, Gallant Lake Resort's cheery yet determined manager, Julie Brown, is a thorn in his side. But the widowed single dad begrudgingly agrees to teach his sassy coworker the game he loves. As their lessons progress, Julie disarms Quinn in ways he can't explain...or ignore. A second chance at love is as rare as a hole in one. Can these rivals at work tee it up for love?

Read on for a sneak peek at
Second-Chance Summer
the next book in the Gallant Lake Stories miniseries
by Jo McNally!

"Look." Quinn's eyes narrowed dangerously. "If this game is that simple, why are you here? If anyone here should feel like they're being punked, it's *me*. You obviously expect to become magically competent at a game you have no respect for without putting in any of the work. I don't know what motivated you to take lessons, but if you're not going to work at it, don't waste my time."

Her whole body went still. Even her lungs seemed to pause. She'd never been good at hearing criticism, especially from men. And Quinn had just used a whole bunch of trigger words. She could hear her mother's voice in her head. *You never listen. You're lazy. Stupid. You want motivation? I'll give you some damn motivation—come here...*

HSEEXP0322

"Julie? Hey, I'm sorry…" Quinn's voice was softer now, edged with regret. She couldn't look at him. She was usually able to control her reactions, but right now she didn't trust herself not to break and either burst into tears or rip into him in a screaming tirade. It had been a long time since she'd done either, but Quinn managed to break through her usual defenses. That realization shook her.

"I've gotta go." She pushed past him, swatting at his hand when he tried to grip her arm. "Don't do that. Just… I need to go. Sorry." She mumbled the last word and kicked herself for it. Apologizing to scolding adults had been her fallback position since she was five. *Sorry, Daddy. Sorry, Mommy. Please don't be mad. Please don't...*

She broke into a near jog toward her car, ignoring Quinn's voice calling after her. He watched in obvious confusion as she drove off. To his credit, he didn't try to stop her. She held herself together until she was off resort property and on the main road, then she cried all the way home. Groceries would have to wait until she could stuff all the ugliness back into the mental vault and pull herself together.

And then she'd have to figure out a way to never, *ever* face Quinn Walker again.